Pineapple

Puzzles

A Pineapple Port Mystery: Book Three

D1522574

Amy Vansant

ISBN: 978-1-5346-1455-0
Library of Congress: 2016909641

Vansant Creations, LLC / Amy Vansant
Annapolis, MD
http://www.AmyVansant.com
http://www.PineapplePort.com

Cover art by Steven Novak.
Copy editing by Carolyn Steele.

DEDICATION

To the cackle twins: Mary & Carol.

CONTENTS

CHAPTER ONE

Two months earlier.

Alex walked into The Striped Goldfish and felt cool, heavy air settling on sun-warmed skin. A skinny man in his mid-fifties sat alone at the bar in a pair of khaki shorts and over-sized Jimmy Buffett t-shirt. In front of him sat a full beer and an empty shot glass. It was three o'clock in the afternoon.

Alex moved to the bar and sat one stool away.

"What can I getcha?" asked the young bartender, his eyes never leaving his phone.

"I'll take a beer. Whatever's on tap."

The bartender finished thumbing his text message, slipped the phone into his pocket and reached to pour a frosted glass.

The man in the Buffet t-shirt spoke.

"Still hot out there?"

"Not too bad. It's been worse," said Alex.

"You aren't kidding. Sometimes I question why I came to Florida in the first place."

"Are you originally from farther north?"

"Isn't everyone? Connecticut."

"Philadelphia, myself."

"See?"

Alex held out a hand. "I'm Alex."

"Pat."

"How long you been here, Pat?"

"In the *bar*, or in Florida?" he asked, chuckling.

"Florida."

"Twenty years. You?"

"Just a few. Retired?"

"I guess you could say I'm semi-retired. I worked for the railroad up in Connecticut. Down here I started making jigsaw puzzles."

"Jigsaw puzzles?"

"Outta wood. I sell them at the craft fairs. Got a website I don't understand. Got some in stores."

"Wait." Alex took a sip of beer. "You're not Pat *Conley* are you?"

Pat grinned. "In the flesh."

"Wow. I've seen your stuff. You're kinda famous. Weren't you and your puzzles on TV or something a few years back?"

"Yeah, well—"

Alex snapped in the air. "Bartender! Get this man another round. Me too, for that matter. I'll have what he's having."

The bartender tucked his tongue into his lower lip, staring as if considering the value of the request, and then nodded.

Alex peppered Pat with questions about the jigsaw puzzle making business and the man answered each inquiry with delight. He never asked about Alex, but then, Alex found most people never thought to steer the conversation away from themselves if given the chance to remain the center of attention.

The shots of bourbon appeared and disappeared like runway models. Alex threw back the first, but for subsequent rounds, dribbled the contents of the shot glass down the leg of the bar stool to the wood plank floor.

It would be important to stay sober.

"I'd sure love to see how you do it," Alex said, as Pat finished expounding on his time creating a puzzle for Mick Jagger's grandchild. Or it might have been James Brown's grandkid. Alex wasn't really listening.

"You should come back to the shop," said Pat, his tongue thick with bourbon.

"Could I? Hey, you need a ride? I have my car."

Pat looked at the door. "I walked here. DUI last year. Lost my license. It was a trap. Cop was *waiting* for me—"

"No problem, no problem. I'll drop you off and you can show me your stuff."

Pat grinned—leered, really—his eyes at half-staff. "Sure sure." He turned to call for the bartender.

"Don't worry about it. I've got the bill."

"This is my kinda day." Pat slid from his bar stool.

Alex paid and palmed Pat's shot glass as the young man ran the card. After signing the receipt Alex held the door open for Pat as they headed for the car. The jigsaw king weaved, giggling at the effort it took to continue forward.

"I might've had one too many today!"

"Happens to the best of us."

Alex opened the passenger door and helped Pat inside. Three minutes later they pulled into the driveway of Pat's moss green, cement block rancher.

After a wobbly trip from the car to the front porch, Pat hummed the theme to *The Brady Bunch* as he fumbled for his keys. The door popped open and they entered.

Inside, the walls were covered with intricate wooden puzzles, assembled, mounted and framed.

"Look at that," said Alex, whistling with admiration.

"That's one of my favorites." Pat thrust his finger in the direction of a large wooden map of the world with each country's puzzle piece stained a slightly different shade. "Took me three years to finish that."

Alex had already wandered to the slider doors leading to the back yard. "No kidding. Is that a pool out there?"

Pat nodded. "You bring your bathing suit?"

"No, but I wouldn't mind sitting out back and getting a little air. Evening breeze is picking up."

He nodded again. "Whatever you like. Grab us some beers from the fridge and I'll lead the way."

Alex gathered one Miller Lite from the fridge and handed the can to Pat before wandering to the edge of the pool.

"Hey Pat!"

Pat, about to flop into a lounge chair, paused. "Yeah?"

"You've got a gator in your pool!"

"What?" Pat shuffled toward the pool. His eyes grew wide. "Hoo!"

In the shallow end of the pool, a large alligator floated, eyes and nose breaking the surface.

"What the—"

Alex opened a pocketknife. Before Pat could say another word, Alex grabbed him by the shoulder of his t-shirt sleeve, stabbed him twice in the neck and pushed him into the pool. The attack took less than three seconds. Not a single drop of blood had fallen on the cement surround.

Pat surfaced sputtering, an ever growing halo of blood encircling his body.

"Did I fall in?" he asked, swimming toward Alex. "Help me out of here!"

He doesn't even realize he's been stabbed. Doesn't know he's bleeding to death faster than he's swimming.

To Alex's surprise, Pat *did* manage to paddle to the edge of the pool. He reached out his hand for help and his mouth opened but he was too weak to speak. Alex watched as the man's eyelids grew heavy. His arm, hooked on the side of the pool, kept Pat afloat, even as his face submerged. It slid in tiny staccato jerks across the pavement as the weight of his body pulled.

A moment later, the alligator was on him. It grabbed Pat by the leg and jerked him under.

Alex stepped forward to watch, curious how the hungry beast would proceed, but the water was too bloody to see.

"I told you if you were patient you'd get fed."

A few details to arrange . . .

Alex returned to the car, retrieved a boxed cardboard puzzle featuring a field of jellybeans, and tossed a handful of pieces in and around the pool.

Alex sat on the end of the lounge chair and watched the pieces bob in the bloody water.

CHAPTER TWO

"This counts towards my detective hours, right?" asked Charlotte.

Sheriff Frank hung his thumbs in his belt and looked at her. "Nah. I just thought you'd like to see a dead guy."

She made a dimple with her right cheek. "Fine. Stupid question."

It might have been a stupid question, but that didn't mean she didn't *want* to see a dead guy. Though, she couldn't see *much* with his face planted firmly in his cereal bowl. She had an excellent view of his bald, sunburned pate. Dead Guy was no spring chicken, but in Charity, Florida, land-of-a-thousand-retirement-communities, very few people were.

She noticed Frank was distracted, messing with his radio, so she poked the dead guy's neck. It was cold. She was about to do it again when she heard Frank.

"Don't."

She looked at him. "Sorry."

He shook his head.

Time to change the subject. "So...heart attack, you think?"

Frank shrugged. He was both the sheriff and one

of her unofficial, adopted fathers. When her grandmother died and left her an orphan, it had been Frank who'd help her keep her grandmother's home in the Pineapple Port fifty-five-plus community *and* avoid social services. Growing up with a whole retirement community for your family was odd, but it was better than shuffling from one group home to the next.

Frank wandered over and studied the back of Dead Guy's head, sucking his tooth with his tongue. He poked his neck, winked at Charlotte, and then grunted.

"Probably is a heart attack. *Though*...I happen to know his wife died two days ago. Might be one of those broken-heart deaths."

"You mean where someone dies because they just can't live without their mate?"

"Yep."

"Aw. That's cute."

"Adorable. Happens more than you'd think. Though I think it has more to do with the shock to their routine than everlasting love. Without Darla I'd starve to death in a week."

Charlotte patted Frank on the arm. "Always such a romantic."

Frank leaned against the refrigerator and stared at the floor. With no knife projecting from the victim's back or brains splattered across the wall, there wasn't much for them to do except wait for the EMTs to arrive and pronounce it death from natural causes.

Or at least as *natural* as death by milk inhalation could be.

Charlotte didn't mind waiting. When she'd asked Frank to help her earn intern hours towards her private detective license, she imagined police work would be exciting. As it turned out, detecting was a lot of standing around. At least this time she was in the same room as an actual Dead Guy.

She wandered toward the back of the house. Nothing appeared out of order. In the bedroom she found a half-empty closet and a pile of women's clothes. Dead Guy must have been organizing his recently deceased wife's things for Goodwill. Her eyes drifted to a faded picture of the couple's children on the bureau.

Dead Guy could have packed up his own stuff while he was at it and saved his kids the trouble.

She chastised herself for thinking such a thing. Growing up in a retirement community had desensitized her to death. Not because she was young and callous; but because her elderly neighbors loved telling sick jokes.

How can you tell your wife died? The sex is the same but the dishes are piling up.

How can you tell your husband died? He finally gets an erection but he doesn't run to tell you about it.

Hear about the old lady with a hole between her breasts? It was her belly button.

She'd heard a million of them.

Charlotte was about to head back to the kitchen when a noise caught her attention. It sounded like someone slowly strangling a balloon to death.

"Was that you, Frank?" she called.

"What's that?"

"Did you make a noise?"

"No. Unless I dozed off. Did it sound like snoring?"

She cocked her head and listened. After a moment the noise began again and continued long enough for her to follow it to the back bedroom. She dropped to her hands and knees and peered under the bed.

Two green eyes peered back at her.

"It's a cat!" she called.

"A what?"

"A *cat*. There's a cat back here. I think it's sick."

Charlotte reached under the bed and the cat batted her hand away. Luckily, it didn't seem to have claws.

"Come on, cat, don't be like that."

She tried again and the cat opened its mouth, threatening to bite.

She skootched forward without fully extending her arm, pretending she couldn't reach as far as she could.

"Here goes nothing," she whispered, taking a moment to summon her courage.

She flicked out her arm like a frog's tongue and grabbed the cat by the back of its neck. A terrifying caterwaul filled the air as she dragged it from beneath the bed.

"Gotcha ya little—*aaah*!"

Charlotte yelped at the sight of the creature in her hand. It took all her power not to toss it away from her.

What had she fished from under the bed?

In the light, it looked less like a cat and more like a baggy, pink rat. The face was feline, but the body was entirely hairless.

"You okay?" called Frank.

"It's some kind of freaky mummy cat!"

"I'm not even going to ask what that means."

The cat struggled briefly and then went limp as she wrapped her arms around it.

The skin didn't feel unlike Dead Guy's, but it was a lot warmer.

She carried the cat to the kitchen.

"I think it's sick," she said, showing Frank the feeble feline cradled against her chest.

Frank made a face as if he'd caught a whiff of something terrible. "Good heavens, that thing is more than *sick*! What is it? Should you be touching it?"

"It's a cat. It's supposed to look like this, I think. It's one of those hairless cats. I hope. But look, it has no energy." She lifted one paw and dropped it. It flopped back into place with no resistance. The cat stared dully up at her with an expression that said, *"I'll let that one slide, but on any other day, I'd kill you for that."*

Frank squinted at it. "I'd give up on life if I looked like that, too."

Charlotte sighed. "I'm going to take it to the vet.

Can I borrow your cruiser? I'll come right back."

Frank rubbed his face with his right hand. "You're killing me."

"Please? It might die."

"It might be evidence."

"You think the *cat* drowned him in his cereal?"

Frank shrugged. "Cats can be pretty sneaky."

Charlotte stared at him until he relented.

"Fine. I'll wait for the ambulance. Go get that thing some Rogaine or something."

Charlotte placed the cat in the passenger seat and drove ten minutes to the local vet clinic. The doctor there said he would see what he could do and give her a call. She was back at the house in less than half an hour. As she pulled up, the EMS techs were rolling a gurney toward the ambulance. A long sheet covered the lump strapped to it.

Bye, Dead Guy.

"Perfect timing," said Frank, standing in the doorway. She threw him the keys to his cruiser and they waited as the body was loaded into the ambulance. As the vehicle pulled away, Charlotte's phone rang and she answered it.

"That was the vet," she said, hanging up a minute later.

"Calling to tell you that's the ugliest cat he's ever seen?"

"No, calling to tell me a quick tox screen says the cat has atropine in its system."

"What's that?"

"He thinks it was poisoned with belladonna."

"The plant?" Frank shook his head. "Cats get into *everything.*"

"Yeah, but don't you think it's weird a cat was poisoned in the same house where two people just *died* in a matter of days?"

Frank was preparing to lock Dead Guy's door and paused. "Now that you mention it..." He re-entered and walked to the cereal bowl. "Maybe we should get this tested."

"Careful, don't touch it without gloves."

"Right. The bowl might have fingerprints on it."

"I was thinking more like it might be *poisonous.*"

"I wasn't going to *taste* it. I don't even like Wheat Chex."

"If it's poison you might not want to get it on your *skin.*"

"Of course not. I was testing you. Good job. You passed." He pulled his hand away from the bowl.

Charlotte scowled.

Riiight.

Frank grimaced and stared at the bowl a moment longer before peeking down the hallway toward the bedrooms.

"If there was enough poison to kill a man, don't you think there would have been enough to kill *ten* cats? How did that hideous cat live and *he* died?"

Charlotte considered this. "His face had a pretty tight fit in that bowl. Maybe the cat could only get to a little milk that splashed when he...splatted."

She reached into her pockets and pulled out a

pair of gloves.

"Look at you, all prepared," said Frank, jerking his radio from his side. The radio crackled to life. "Ruby?"

"I'm here, Sheriff," said Ruby from her station at the sheriff's office. She'd replaced Miss Charlene, who'd moved to Alabama.

"Can you get me a tech out here to 745 Locust Ave? I need something tested for poison and I don't want to touch it."

"Is it poop?"

"What?"

"You said you don't wanna touch it. Is it poop?"

"No, Ruby, it is *not* poop."

"Alrighty then. Yes sir, I certainly will get you a tech."

Charlotte looked at Frank as he replaced his radio, head shaking.

"Was she *not* going to get you a tech if it *was* poop?" she asked.

He sighed. "She's getting weirder every day, I swear. I'm starting to wonder if recommending Ruby was Charlene's final revenge before she left."

Charlotte chuckled and opened the refrigerator. She was surprised to find room in it. All the people she knew in Pineapple Port kept their fridges overflowing with food. If anything was on special Mariska always had to buy six. Between meal leftovers, recipes ripped from *Woman's World* magazine and shared neighborhood baked goods, Mariska couldn't squeeze another grape in her fridge with a shoehorn.

Charlotte pulled the milk carton from the refrigerator with her gloved hand and put it next to the bowl on the table for testing. Peering back into the fridge, she noticed a white powder on the top shelf near the back. She removed some orange juice and a few more items to get a better view.

"You making a snack?" asked Frank.

"There's a white powder on the shelf."

"Well, let the techs deal with it. Don't mess with anything. You might inhale something."

Charlotte put her hand over her face, realized her glove might have already touched the powder and whipped it away.

She was about to stop pretending she had any idea what she was doing, when she noticed a shallow, square indentation in the back wall of the fridge. She poked it, but it didn't move. Running her gloved finger over it, she found it slid to the side and sprung back into place. She tried again, applying more pressure. This time the little trapdoor revealed what looked like the end of a plastic tube. She stared at it. This wasn't a refrigerator feature with which she was familiar. She allowed the trap door to snap shut again.

"Frank, there is something really weird back here."

"You wouldn't believe what old people eat sometimes. I remember Darla got on this prune and wheatgrass kick—"

"No, I mean there's a secret door in the back of

their fridge."

"What?"

Frank peered in and Charlotte showed him how the door slid to the side and sprang back into place.

He tapped her on the shoulder to get her to move and closed the door. He walked to the side and, with great effort, slid the refrigerator away from the wall.

He peeked behind it. "What the heck is that?"

Charlotte shifted to get a better view. There was a small water bottle taped to the back of the refrigerator with a tube running from the bottom to the sliding door. The trap door was a piece of white plastic with a spring and a plastic loop on the opposite side. Clear fishline was tied to the loop and led to the other side of the fridge, out of view.

Charlotte circled the appliance and spotted the line protruding from the other side. She pulled the coffee pot in the corner of the counter toward her to investigate.

"What did you just do? The door opened," said Frank.

Charlotte looked at the back of the coffee machine and found the fishline ended there, secured to the back. She flipped the top and peered inside to confirm that was where someone making coffee would pour water.

She pushed the coffee machine back into its corner.

"Now the door is closed," said Frank.

Charlotte opened the refrigerator and pulled the

coffee maker toward her again. She watched the sliding door open.

She grabbed the carton of milk from the table and put it back in the refrigerator. She eyeballed its height, and found the top of the carton sat just beneath the hole.

"I think they poisoned themselves," said Charlotte.

"You think they built a contraption to poison themselves on *purpose?*"

"No, I think someone else built a contraption to *trick* them into poisoning themselves. Someone put poison powder in that tube and rested it against that little door. They must have put the milk directly under it with the spout open. The next morning these poor people pulled out their coffee machine so they could flip open the top and pour in the water. When they did, it pulled the fishline and released the powder into the open carton."

"These people didn't notice their milk was open?"

Charlotte put her hands on her hips. "If you found your milk open in the fridge, would you start looking for a poison delivery system?"

Frank shook his head. "No, I guess not. I'd probably just blame Darla."

"Exactly."

He pointed. "I think you just put your poison gloves on your hips."

Charlotte realized she was resting the knuckles of each hand on her hips and held out her arms.

"Shoot."

"So finish your theory," said Frank.

She sighed, holding her hands a safe distance from her body. "Once they poured the water into the coffee machine, they probably pushed it back. The hole snapped shut and they didn't notice it."

Frank grimaced. "That's a pretty good theory, assuming the milk is poisoned. We'd better take the orange juice too, just in case."

Charlotte nodded. "They'll probably want to test a lot of stuff, but my money is on the milk. There's no coffee in the pot so maybe the man didn't drink it. I'm thinking the missus took milk in her coffee, so she died first. Then a couple days later the husband decided to have cereal and...*sploosh*."

"Is that the sound of a man dying in his *Wheaties*? *Sploosh*?"

She nodded. "*Duh*." She pulled the gloves from her hands and put them next to the milk. "Who would do something like this?"

She looked at Frank, who stood frozen, staring at nothing. "Frank?"

Frank frowned. "I'm afraid I know *exactly* who would do something like this."

He opened the refrigerator and scanned it, moving the contents left and right as if looking for something. Finally, he opened the butter compartment and gasped.

"What is it?" asked Charlotte.

He grabbed her gloves from the table and, slipping one on, gently pulled something from behind a box of butter sticks. He held it up for her to see.

It was a piece from a common cardboard jigsaw puzzle.

Charlotte squinted at it and recognized the pattern printed on it.

"Jellybeans?" she asked.

CHAPTER THREE

The bell connected to the Hock o' Bell Pawnshop's door rang its merry greeting and Declan looked up to see who'd entered. He realized part of him worried it was the man he'd just hired part-time. *Blade.* Something about the guy was a little unsettling. Maybe that his name was Blade. That should have been his first clue. He was already wondering if he'd made the right decision between Blade and paying for another month of want ads in the local paper. *Something about that guy—*

Declan's apprehensions over his hiring practices dissipated as he watched a blonde in a tight blue business suit slink through the door.

Oh no.

This was much worse. Now his heart yearned for Blade.

It was *Stephanie* darkening his door. His ex. Growing up with her had blinded him to the horror of dating her and, like a fool, he'd given it a shot.

She made Blade look like Santa Claus.

Who knew when he started a pawnshop the greatest downside would be that his ex-girlfriend could pop in any time she wanted?

"Why?" he asked, dropping his gaze to continue

his paperwork.

"Why what?" she asked, weaving through the furniture. He'd recently reconfigured his wares, forcing people to walk through more of them on their way to the counter. Not only did it help sales (theoretically), it also kept bad guys from bolting straight from his counter to the door, which hadn't been a problem until recently.

"Why are you *here*?"

"Oh. Nice to see you, too, *Decky*."

Declan's gaze rose from his books. The sound of her pet name for him made his blood run cold. She stopped at the counter and smiled at him.

She had a face that launched a thousand trips...*to therapists.*

She sighed. "You blinked first but I'll get to the point. Doesn't your little friend work with the police or something?"

"My little friend?"

"*Whatsherface.*"

"You mean my *girlfriend*? Charlotte?"

"Mm. Whatever. I don't like labeling people."

"She's training to be a detective, if that's what you mean."

Stephanie grimaced. "Oh. I thought she was more than that. A cop or something. Probably the total lack of femininity about her gave me that impression."

"You're pushing it. Get to the point."

"Oh! I know. She's friends with the sheriff, isn't she?"

"Yes. He's helping her get her license."

"Good. I need you to give her a message to give to him."

Declan sighed. "I don't know where this is going but I already don't like it."

"Tell her to tell him there's a serial killer in town."

Declan's eyes grew wide. "What? Why would I do that?"

"Because there is."

"No, I mean why wouldn't *you* tell the police if you know there's a serial killer in town?"

She shook her head. "It's for a client. I can't answer any questions about it and don't want to draw attention. Lawyer-client privilege and all that."

"You take serial killers for clients?"

"My client isn't the serial killer. Not that I could tell you if she was."

"This is ridiculous. Just send them an anonymous note or something."

"Too slow. I need you to be our official go between. And there's another side to this: We need any information Charlotte and Sheriff get on the case. In return, we'll give you any information we get. Sounds like a sitcom, doesn't it? *Charlotte and Sheriff?*"

He scowled. "Is this another excuse to talk to me?"

Stephanie flipped her hair with one exaggerated toss of her head. "Don't flatter yourself."

"You already told me you were going to stalk me until you got me back. I don't think it's a stretch to suspect this nonsense is part of your plan."

"It's not. And if I had a plan you'd never know it."

"Probably not," he muttered.

"Look..." Stephanie put her hand on the counter in front of him. "You should know that this case involves you and Charlotte. More than I can tell you. If you don't help, you could be putting your own lives in danger."

Declan opened his mouth to protest, but Stephanie put her finger on his lips before spinning on her heel and weaving her way toward the exit.

"Wait! What's that supposed to mean?" he called after her.

She huffed. "This ridiculous furniture configuration is like a roller coaster line in Disney World."

He tried again. He had time, thanks to the furniture maze. "Steph! How are *we* involved?"

She raised her hand to wave and left without another word.

Declan retrieved his phone and called Charlotte.

"Hello cutie," she answered.

"Where are you?"

"Hello Declan!" he heard Mariska sing-song in the background. Wherever Charlotte was, chances were good that Mariska and Sheriff Frank's wife, Darla, were nearby.

"I'm in a car on our way to pick up Mariska's sister at the airport."

"Is Frank with you?"

"No. Why would Frank be with us?"

"I guess he wouldn't. I have a message for you that you're supposed to give him."

"From whom?"

"That's just it, I'm not supposed to tell you. Though I probably will. Give me a little time though to think about it."

"How mysterious."

He grunted. "Mm. You know me. Mr. Mysterious."

"Tall, dark and mysterious," said Mariska, giggling.

"You forgot *handsome*," said Charlotte.

"Oh, that goes without saying. He's got those cute little buns—"

Declan felt himself blush. There was a kerfuffle on the line as he imagined Charlotte was trying to shush Mariska, who only giggled all the harder.

After a moment, Charlotte's voice returned. "Sorry. So what's the message?"

"Tell Frank there's a serial killer in town."

"What's that supposed to mean?"

"I think it means *there's a serial killer in town.*"

"It's not, like...code or something?"

"Why would it be code? I think someone is warning him that there's an actual serial killer in town."

The phone fell silent.

"Charlotte?"

"I'm here. Did this mysterious person that is

probably almost definitely Stephanie say anything about milk?"

"Steph—" Declan paused and cleared his throat. "I told you I can't say who it is. What's this about *milk*? She didn't say anything else about anything."

"*She?*"

"Or he."

"Uh huh."

"She or he. I might have been trying to throw you off by saying she. Maybe it's none of the above."

"Not *he* or *she*? Did a brown bear stop by and warn you not to cause forest fires and oh—there's a serial killer in town? Maybe a star-nosed mole popped up out of the floor and whispered it to you?"

"Ha ha. Fine. It was a human being. More or less. That's all I'm saying for now."

"And that's it? I need to tell Frank there's a serial killer in town?"

Declan heard Mariska's voice in the background ask: *There's a what?*

"Yep. And don't tell him I told you, I guess."

"You guess?"

"I don't know how many levels of secrecy there are supposed to be, but I guess the more the merrier. I'll talk to you more about it later."

"Did you say *serial killer?*" repeated Mariska. Charlotte hushed her.

"You know by telling me this with Mariska in the car, you've ensured everyone within a fifty mile radius will know about it."

"Oh, that isn't true," huffed Mariska. "But he *did*

say serial killer, didn't he?"

Declan smiled. "I'll remember that for the next time I have mysterious information for you."

"Fine. But I have to tell you, you're terrible at this. And I *will* talk to you more about this later."

He sighed. "I know."

CHAPTER FOUR

"I know that grunt." Charlotte hung up the phone and looked at Mariska. "That was his *Stephanie* grunt."

"What? *Who*? Declan?"

"Uh huh. He has this grunt he makes when he's referencing the Viper."

"Stephanie?"

She nodded. "It sounds like someone just stabbed him in the liver."

"And he made that grunt? Why?"

"I don't think I'm allowed to say."

Mariska tapped her on the leg. "You said serial killer. Is *Stephanie* a serial killer?"

"No. I hope not. That would bode poorly for me."

"You're not kidding. You're the only thing standing between her and Declan."

"*Me* and the fact that he'd rather be covered in jelly and staked to an ant hill than date that harpy again."

Mariska laughed. "*Staked to an anthill.* Where does your mind come up with these things? And why is she so obsessed with him, anyway? I mean, he's built like a Greek god, but—"

"Mariska!"

"What?"

Charlotte sighed. "Stop talking about my boyfriend like he's a steak and you're starving."

This sent Mariska into peals of laughter. "Can I get some A1 with that?"

Charlotte tried not to laugh, and failed.

She pulled into the airport's cell phone lot to wait for Mariska's sister Carolina to call and alert them to her safe landing.

Mariska opened her phone. She didn't text very often and still owned a flip phone, so it took her a good ten minutes to send her sister a notice saying *We are here.*

"I couldn't figure out the apostrophe to say *we're* so I told her *we are here* which took more letters," she said, snapping the phone shut. She looked exhausted.

"That'll do, I'm sure."

Mariska turned to her. "So what was all that about a serial killer? Is it the milk poisoner you told me about?"

Charlotte shrugged. "I suppose. That seems like the most serial-killery thing that's happened around here lately, doesn't it?"

"You said Frank knew who did it."

"He thought it might be the Puzzle Killer, someone who was killing in this area years ago. Frank thinks he's back."

"Why do they call him the Puzzle Killer?"

"Because he never just *kills* someone. It's always

an elaborate ordeal. Frank said they were calling him the Rube Goldberg killer for a while, but not everyone got the reference and the cops were getting confused."

"Goldberg was the traitor, right?"

"No, you're thinking of the Rosenbergs. Rube Goldberg drew pictures of elaborate machines that did simple things. See? Puzzle Killer is just easier."

"Definitely. I knew a Barbie Goldberg, but I don't think she'd kill anyone..."

Mariska's phone rang and she answered. Five minutes later she hung up.

"Is she delayed?"

"No, she's on the curb ready to go."

"The whole time you were talking to her she was *on the curb*?"

Mariska nodded. "All the peanuts in her bag were half burnt and the lady next to her wouldn't stop moving her elbow past the half way point and the man on the other side of her had a cough."

"And she couldn't wait until she was in the car to tell you that?"

"It was all pretty upsetting. Apparently, the worst part about the cough was that the guy kept trying to *keep* from coughing, so when he did it was like an explosion."

Mariska giggled as Charlotte rubbed her face with her hand and tried to mentally prepare herself. When Mariska and her sister got together it was always a giggle fest. She called them the Cackle Twins, because once they got to cackling, there was no end to it.

She hadn't seen Carolina for a couple of years and was looking forward to it, but coming back to her now was *how* opinionated Mariska's sister could be. For every judgement Mariska had, Carolina had two. Between that and the giggling, it was shaping up to be quite a visit.

They spotted Carolina at the curb with three suitcases nearly as tall as she was. She waved to catch their attention, her blonde bob rocking with the motion.

Charlotte looked at Mariska. "How long is she staying? A *year*?"

"Two weeks."

"And *three* suitcases? She could pack bodies in those things."

"One's probably empty so she can take things back home."

They parked and both hopped out to help Carolina with her bags. Charlotte waited her turn and then hugged her hello.

"Bring enough luggage?" she asked. She'd promised herself she wouldn't, but it came out of her mouth anyway.

"One's empty so I can take some orange juice home."

Charlotte squinted at her. "Does the entire state of Michigan have scurvy?"

Carolina looked at her, emotionless. "You're so *weird*."

Charlotte opened her mouth and then shut it.

There were *so* many arguments as to why packing a suitcase full of orange juice was a bad idea, but she had to let it slide.

Let it slide. Let it slide...

They threw Carolina's luggage in the back of Mariska's car and headed for Pineapple Port by way of a restaurant in St. Pete Beach.

"It's *hot*," said Carolina as they sat at a plastic table beneath a faux palm-frond roof. "Why would you live in this wretched furnace of a state? It isn't natural unless you're a snake."

"Take off your sweatshirt," suggested Mariska.

Carolina wrapped her arms around her shoulders. "It was so cold on that plane I thought they'd have to remove my *feet* by the time I got here. My toes are probably *black*. One way or another I'm going to lose my feet. I know it. If it isn't the darn diabetes it'll be the cold planes."

"Well, you're not on the plane, now. Take it off."

"If I take off my sweatshirt my pits will be all sweaty thanks to the fact you live in a giant sweat lodge."

A woman sitting at the next table shot Carolina a look. Charlotte offered her an apologetic smile.

She wasn't sure why Carolina's pits would be sweaty if she was freezing on the plane...but it was probably something about old age she didn't want to know. She already knew too much.

Mariska tugged on the arm of her sister's sweatshirt. "They'll dry. You can just hold your arms up for a bit and let the pits air out."

The woman at the other table glanced their way again. This time Charlotte stuck her tongue out at her, just a little bit.

The woman turned back to her table in a huff and Charlotte smiled at Carolina.

"Yeah, just flap those arms around. Let those pits really *breathe*."

"I'll look like I'm doing the chicken dance," muttered Carolina.

"The chicken dance!" echoed Mariska, beginning to giggle.

"Oh no. Here we go," said Charlotte, dropping back her head to stare at the ceiling.

When her neck started to ache she looked back up to find Carolina half out of her sweatshirt, trapped with one arm and her head still inside. Mariska was humming the Chicken Dance.

"Doodle doodle doodle do, Doodle doodle doodle do, Doodle doodle doodle do!" She clapped four times, noticed her sister was trapped in the sweatshirt and howled with laughter.

"It's not funny, help me out of this thing!" came Carolina's muffled voice.

Mariska stood and helped pull the sweatshirt off her now hysterical sister and the two of them rocked back and forth in their chairs, half cackling and half chicken dancing.

"Can I buy you ladies a cocktail?"

A small, grinning older man approached the table and set up camp between the Cackle Sisters. His skinny legs supported a pair of plaid shorts, held aloft by a leather belt that disappeared beneath his pot belly. He rubbed his short, steel-gray hair awaiting their response.

Carolina squinted one eye at the man.

"What are you up to?" she asked. She turned to Mariska. "What is he up to?"

"I think he wants to buy us a drink," said Mariska. She looked at the man. "But we're good, thank you."

"The last thing these two need is a drink," said Charlotte, trying to fill the gap where politeness had failed Auntie Carolina.

"It seemed like you were having quite a party over here," he said. "I'm Lester Swander."

He held out his hand to Carolina, who grunted and folded her sweatshirt into her lap.

"Well...I'll see you around. You ladies have a nice day." He offered one last nod and wandered off.

As soon as he was gone Mariska looked at Charlotte. "Didn't he look familiar? I think he might be that fellow who's renting in the old section."

"At Pineapple Port?"

Mariska nodded.

"Well, I don't know who he thinks he is; him and those *teeth*," said Carolina. "Looks like he's stolen some poor horse's chompers."

"Oh *didn't* he have beautiful teeth?" said Mariska.

"You've got to be kidding. I was afraid he was going to *bite* me. He might have taken off my arm."

"Think of the air that would hit your pits then," mumbled Charlotte. *Was it too early for a drink? Nah...*

Mariska shook her head. "I think he just wanted to buy you a drink because you looked like fun."

"*Looked like fun*," Carolina echoed. "How awful."

"He only had eyes for you. I think it's those enormous knockers of yours," Mariska added, giggling again.

Carolina shot her a look and then chuckled. "They've always been a problem."

"Mind of their own!"

The two women put hands on each other's arms, and Charlotte worried they would suffocate laughing.

CHAPTER FIVE

One Month Earlier.

The Future Horizons Alzheimer's home kept its door locked. At first Alex thought that was odd, but older, confused people *did* tend to wander. The home had to keep the door locked so the residents didn't ramble outside and disappear into a swamp.

Locked doors were good for the residents, but a problem for people trying to sneak inside. There would be no slipping into the building. It wouldn't be like wandering into a hospital and blending in with the other visitors; all those good people *not* planning to kill someone.

Alex stood in the parking lot watching people knock on the home's door. They always gained entry without trouble, thanks to the distracted nurses rolling wheelchairs through the vestibule. The nurse would stop rolling his or her patient around like a room service cart, open the door, and continue on, sometimes without a word exchanged. There was no *real* security. People came to visit their loved ones and whoever happened to be near the door let them in, no questions asked. Nobody asked to see I.D. or demanded visitors prove they were family members.

After all, who would pretend they were related to an Alzheimer patient? What would be the point? You couldn't wheedle your way into the will of somebody who couldn't remember who you were from one day to the next.

The door swung open and a couple left the center, the man's burly arm wrapped around the woman's thick shoulders. The woman wiped tears from her eyes as they wobbled to the car, bobbing against each other, connected in their loving but awkward way.

"My own mother doesn't even remember me," said the woman, her voice cracking.

"It's a terrible thing," said the man.

Alex approached the couple, smiling.

"I know you two... Aren't you Olivia's kids?"

The couple stopped and the woman put her hand against her chest. "Us? No, I'm Stacy—Andrea Longo's daughter."

"Oh, I'm *so* sorry. You look something like Olivia's daughter. I apologize."

Alex offered a nod of apology and headed toward the home.

Andrea Longo. If anyone asked any questions, Alex was there to see *Andrea Longo.* Andrea wouldn't be able to confirm or deny; judging from her daughter's tears, Andrea Longo's mind was wandering somewhere far, far away.

Alex knocked on the door and a nurse pushing a woman with a million-yard stare opened it. Alex thanked her and headed toward the hallway as if the way was familiar.

The patients' names were on their doors.

How convenient.

It didn't take long to find the right room; the room with the paper insert in a brass frame that read *Roger Stekel.*

Best to print the names out on paper; one never knew how often they might have to be changed.

Alex knocked, heard no response, and slipped inside the room.

"Wow."

Roger's room was wallpapered with finished crossword puzzles. Now ninety years old, Roger Stekel had completed one crossword puzzle per day for the last sixty years.

That was one way to kill a life.

Roger napped, a half-finished puzzle rising and falling on his chest, a pen still in his fingers.

The pen gave Alex an idea.

"I'm going to need you to sit up for me, Mr. Stekel."

Roger didn't move.

Grabbing both of Roger's pajama lapels, Alex tugged on the old man and sat him upright. He pulled back the blankets and swiveled each of the old man's legs in turn, hanging them over the side of the bed.

"Can you walk Roger?"

Roger's lids fluttered. "What?" he croaked.

"Can you walk?"

The old man grimaced. "Of course I can walk!"

Better check. A pinch to Roger's veiny calf made the puzzle master jump.

"Ow!"

"Sorry about that. I can't risk you not being able to get out of bed on your own."

"What? Who are you?"

Alex put an arm around the old man's back and wrapped a hand around Roger's, holding rigid the pen still balanced in his liver-spotted hand.

"Sorry about this, Rog."

"What?"

In one swift movement, Alex jerked Roger's pen-holding hand, stabbing the crossword king in the jugular and pushing his body forward. Roger landed on his knees and forehead, blood pooling on the low-pile carpet. He didn't make a sound as he slowly collapsed to one side.

Alex pictured the headlines:

Local puzzle-solving master falls out of bed and stabs himself with his puzzle-solving pen.

Oh, the irony.

Perfect. The jackals at the news outlets loved irony.

His death would make the news.

Alex pulled a puzzle piece from his pocket and slipped it under Roger's head, careful not to knock over the body. Alex slipped from the room and, after a panicked moment searching the walls for a code to unlock the exit to the building, strolled back into sunlight.

CHAPTER SIX

Seamus stared at the stuffed bear holding a chocolate, heart-shaped lollypop. *Would Jackie like that? She might. She likes chocolate. But she'd never mentioned bears one way or the other...*

He sighed and wondered how he could be so bad at romance. He thought of himself as a romantic guy, but none of his exes seemed to agree in the end. His nephew Declan always knew how to delight the ladies. The young buck had given Charlotte an HDMI cable for her television and she'd giggled like he was a knight returning from a dragon's lair with the Holy Grail.

What was that about? More importantly...

Would Jackie *like a cable?*

Nah. She didn't even watch much television.

He picked up the bear.

"That's leftover stock from Valentine's Day," said a voice with a French accent.

He turned and found the tall, dark-haired Simone standing behind him, smiling like a hungry fox. Seamus felt like a baby chick dropped from the nest. Simone was his age, mid-fifties, but her sex appeal was timeless. The last time he'd run into

Simone she'd handcuffed him to her wall. He'd barely made it out with his fidelity to Jackie intact, because while the handcuff stuff wasn't his thing, *it wasn't uninteresting*. And Simone *wasn't unattractive*.

"It's nearly Thanksgiving," he said, finding that his saliva had packed up and left town.

"Exactly," she said, taking the bear from him. "Unless it's a chew toy for your dog, you can do better than a drugstore bear."

"I think a drugstore bear would be unsafe for a dog. Toxic stuffing and whatnot."

"Not my point."

"Fair enough."

She leaned across him to return the bear to its dusty home. Her breasts brushed his arm. She smelled like a champagne brunch on the back of a yacht anchored off of Monaco. He could picture the scene—water sparkling in the morning sun, calla lilies in a glass vase on the table—

Boy, she was good.

"It was a joke gift," he muttered, taking a strategic step back.

"I'm sure."

"So...how have you been?"

She bit her lower lip and stared into his eyes before speaking. "I've been better. I need your help."

"*My* help?"

"You fancy yourself a detective, correct?"

"I don't know if *fancy* is the word. It's what I do. There's nothing fancy about it."

"I need you to find someone."

"One of your witness protection people?"

Simone's eyes grew wide and she grabbed the front of his shirt. "How do you know about that?" she asked, her French accent replaced by something much less exotic.

Seamus held up his hands and grinned. He didn't want to tell her he'd heard about how she'd been banished by the Federal Marshals for sending a large number of criminals under witness protection to the same area of Florida. *This area of Florida.* She'd been reassigned to babysit her "clients" and make sure witnesses from rival criminal enterprises didn't clash in the local Publix.

He knew things she didn't know he knew. He grinned. For the first time he didn't feel off balance talking to Simone and he liked it.

"I told you; I'm a private investigator. I know a lot of things."

She let him go and smoothed his shirt.

"Sorry. People die when my secrets become public."

Feeling cocky, Seamus put his hand on his hip and stretched his other arm to prop himself against the shelves. As he applied his weight, the shelf popped up and he fell against the shelving unit. Several heart bears and a dozen plastic tubes of knock-off M&Ms spilled to the ground. He scrambled to retrieve them and threw them back on the shelf as quickly as they rolled off a second and third time.

When he'd managed to balance everything on

the shelf, he noticed Simone staring at him, her arms crossed against her chest.

He cleared his throat. "So how can I help?"

"I think one of my witnesses has gone rogue. I need to find him."

"Can't you call in the Marshals for this?"

Simone sighed. "I think they're upset enough with me."

"Okay. So what's this rogue's name?"

"I don't know."

"You don't *know?*"

She shook her head. "I don't know who it is."

"So this person could be a man, woman or head of cabbage? How is that possible? How can *you* not know the person *you* put into Witsec?"

"Shhh..." she said, covering his mouth with her hand. "Lower your voice. Someone is killing people and I'm worried it's one of my clients. They aren't the most upstanding group of people, you know."

"Killing who?"

"Did you read about the man eaten by an alligator in his pool? It was two months ago."

Seamus nodded. "You're saying he *wasn't* eaten by an alligator? The enormous reptile in his pool was a coincidence?"

"I'm saying I think the alligator was *placed* there to make it *look* like an accident. There was a crossword champion, too, a month back. Only his obituary was in the paper, but I discovered they found him on the ground with his puzzle pen *embedded in his aorta.*"

"And that didn't raise any flags with the police?"

"It looked as though he'd fallen on it. They ruled it an accident. I think the two are connected. It's my job to find links in situations like these."

"So you want me to find a fella who's killed two people in the last two months and that's all the information you can give me?"

"The victims were both puzzle enthusiasts."

"Oh, *great* intel. If I can identify the next victim he can help me finish my clear blue sky before he's brutally murdered. Anything else?"

Simone shook her head. The point of her dark, bobbed hair touched one edge of her mouth and then the other. Her full lips were brilliant crimson. Seamus looked away to keep himself from staring. In his head, he rattled off the last five winners of the FIFA cup and then returned his attention to Simone.

The power women had over men was nothing less than black magic.

"What's the pay?" he asked.

"You require money?"

"That's how these things usually work."

She moved closer to him "There are other ways."

He stepped back. "Money would be just fine."

She smiled. "How's two thousand?"

Seamus tried not to react to what he thought was an overly generous offer. "Identification or identification and capture?"

"Identification."

He ran his tongue over his teeth, considering.

"Expenses?"

"Let me know if it runs more than five hundred. Try not to use all of it."

"Two thousand four hundred and ninety-nine it is then," he said, holding out his hand.

She shook.

"Make it quick," she said, turning on her four inch black heel and striding down the aisle.

He took a deep breath and watched her walk before cursing quietly under his breath.

He'd forgotten to ask her what he *should* buy Jackie.

CHAPTER SEVEN

Every morning the girl came out of her house and walked her dog around the neighborhood.

Charlotte.

How could a young woman have such a pretty name?

Charlotte.

He studied her from behind the bushes as she clipped the leash on to her dog's collar and started down the steps. Her long, tan legs covered ground quickly, and soon he had to move to continue watching her walk down the street.

Charlotte.

She never locked her door before leaving. No one in the neighborhood locked their door, but that didn't matter to him. He'd never steal from any of the people of Pineapple Port. He wasn't a thief. And ninety-nine percent of the time, he'd never creep into their homes and lay in their beds while they were out walking their dogs. He would never stare at their underwear lying in a drawer. He would never tremble at the thought of touching them...

That was ninety-nine percent of the time.

Charlotte was the exception. She was the one percent who had captured his heart.

Charlotte was a *goddess*.

Her pillow smelled like honey. Sometimes he'd open her bureau drawers and stare at her bras and panties. He hadn't touched them yet. Not yet. Maybe today would be the day. He felt brave.

He almost took one once, a pink pair of panties with lace around the top edge, but before he could find the courage, he realized he'd lingered too long and barely made it out before she and the dog returned.

Today he thought that, before he slipped under the sheets of her unmade bed, he'd check the refrigerator for leftovers. He wanted to find a spot where she'd bitten and bite there, too.

Oh those lips.

To have his lips so close to hers...

Charlotte.

CHAPTER EIGHT

Charlotte returned from her walk and unclipped her soft-coated Wheaton terrier's leash. Abby-dog bolted down the hall and ran around the house, sniffing every room as if a squirrel had taken up residence during her absence.

"Are you crazy?" Charlotte asked, shaking her head. The dog had been doing a post-walk gallop around the house for months and she had no idea how the odd behavior started. The dog toured the house a few times, sniffing furiously, then plunked herself down on Charlotte's side of the bed to roll around.

She assumed Abby had done it *once* for a reason only her dog brain knew, and now it was a pattern. Dogs could be very OCD that way.

After dressing, Charlotte said goodbye to her loon of a dog, who had since curled up for her nap on the bed. She went outside to retrieve her bike and pedaled her way to Declan's house, a few blocks north and east of Pineapple Port. He'd recently hired someone to watch his pawnshop and for the first time in a long time, had a whole day off.

She leaned her bike against his garage door and bounced to the porch. She knocked, giddy with the possibility of a day alone with Declan. As long as his uncle Seamus wasn't—

The door opened.

"Hello there, Miss Charlotte!"

Charlotte sighed.

"Hi, Seamus."

So much for our romantic day alone.

Seamus stepped aside to allow her entry and she permitted her expression to fall for the briefest of moments before jerking the corners of her mouth back into a smile.

She spotted Declan in the kitchen.

"If it isn't Mister Leisure," she said.

Declan grinned, his gorgeous green eyes rolling.

"Turns out there's nothing leisurely about leaving your livelihood in the hands of a stranger," he said, offering her a peck on the lips. "I'm a nervous wreck."

"You don't trust your new hire?"

He shrugged. "I trust him. He's just...*weird*. Plus, the store is my baby, so it's hard."

"I've had to keep him from rushing down there all morning," said Seamus, moving to his seat at the kitchen table and picking up his newspaper.

"What are you doing here, Seamus?" she asked, eyeing Declan. He mouthed *sorry* to her.

"I'm giving Jackie a bit of a breather. I think my constant presence in her home was a *wee* bit annoying for her. She's set in her ways, you know. Not a fan of bears, either."

Charlotte squinted at him but he didn't seem to

feel any need to explain the bear comment. "No luck on your house hunt?"

Seamus had been threatening to find a home of his own for months.

"Nothing yet."

"Completely for lack of trying," muttered Declan.

Declan's uncle attempted to fold his paper, gave up, and placed the crinkled mess on the table beside him. "I was also hoping to catch you here."

Charlotte pointed to her chest. "Me?"

"I knew if my boy had a day off, you wouldn't be far behind." Seamus winked and Declan glared at him.

"What's up?" she asked.

"You're still working with Frank, right? Working toward your P.I. license?"

She nodded. "Yes. You've been no help lately."

He offered her a lopsided smile. "True, the detecting business has been a bit slow for me lately, but I *do* have something I thought you might be able to help me with. You or Frank know anything about a serial killer in town?"

Declan had wandered to the sink to clean up the breakfast dishes left by his uncle, but at the sound of *serial killer* his head snapped up and he exchanged a look with Charlotte.

Seamus didn't miss it.

"What's this now? Why are you looking at each other like a couple of creepy twins? The kind with that special language only they share..."

Declan looked at Charlotte. "Should I go first or should you tell your milk story?"

Charlotte leaned against the wall. "I don't know how much I'm supposed to share with laypeople."

Seamus straightened in his chair. "Come on, lass, spill. Tell your old uncle Seamus what you know and free yourself from that dark, terrible secret, eatin' at your soul."

Charlotte chuckled. She couldn't resist Seamus when he poured on the Irish charm.

"You know the couple who died one day after each other? Police said they suspected poison?" she said.

"Over in Paradise Park? Aye, I read about them in the paper."

"*My* paper," said Declan, striding over and attempting to refold the paper his uncle had balled on the table.

Charlotte waited a moment for the crinkling to stop. Declan caught her staring at him.

"Sorry. He's like some kind of origami idiot savant." He stopped, the mess still in his hands.

She continued. "Well, there was a contraption that poisoned them."

"A contraption?"

"There was fishing line tied to their coffee machine. When they pulled it out to open the top and pour in the water, the string triggered a door on the back of the fridge and poison in a tube slid out into their milk."

"Really?" the two men said in unison.

"That's...*ridiculous*," added Declan.

"It sounds like the Puzzle Killer," mumbled Seamus.

Charlotte pointed at him. "Yes! That's what Frank said. And he found a puzzle piece in the butter compartment of the fridge. You know about the Puzzle Killer?"

Seamus nodded. "Twenty-odd years ago, when I was still in the area, he was knockin' off people here and there, but he never just *killed* anyone. There always had to be a trick to it."

"Like this contraption?" said Declan.

"Exactly," said Charlotte. "Frank's since told me the milk tested positive for atropine—belladonna poison—just like the cat."

"What *cat*?"

"Oh, yeah. I have a cat."

"*You* have a cat?"

"Temporarily. We found the dead guy with his face in a bowl of cereal and the cat was *nearly* dead from trying to clean up the mess. It's why we figured the milk was responsible."

"I didn't read about this trap door in the paper," said Seamus.

"I think they wanted to keep that detail a secret. Maybe they didn't want people to panic over the idea a famous serial killer is back in town."

Declan abandoned refolding the paper and instead walked it to the trashcan and stuffed it inside. "Does killing a married couple make you a serial killer? Sounds more like someone wanted *them* dead and they just had a weird way of doing it."

Charlotte agreed. "Maybe someone is trying to pin it on the Puzzle Killer, but really, they just wanted *that* couple dead."

"Here's where I can pay you back with a little information of my own," said Seamus. "Simone thinks two other murders are connected to each other. Maybe this one is connected as well."

Charlotte scowled. "*Simone*. Why is that name familiar?"

"Isn't that the woman who sent Rocky?" asked Declan.

Seamus nodded.

The three of them had recently met a man who, thanks to witness protection, lived in the area. All the people he'd ratted on were dead, so he hadn't minded confessing his situation to them.

"Does she think it's one of her people committing the murders?" asked Charlotte.

"She thinks the deaths of a crossword champ and Mr. Alligator Bait might be the work of one of her people, yes. She doesn't have a lot of faith in her clients to be good people."

"Mr. Alligator Bait?" asked Declan.

"Fella was gobbled by an alligator in his pool about a month ago," said Seamus.

Declan's eyes grew wide and his gaze swiveled to where his lap pool sat outside his sliding glass doors. "How'd I miss that one?"

"Who's the crossword champ?" asked Charlotte.

"Man in an Alzheimer's home fell out of bed and

took a pen to the throat," said Seamus. "Except Simone thinks it wasn't an accident. Doesn't think the alligator just wandered in for a swim, either."

"Why? What makes them suspicious deaths?"

He shrugged. "She has access to Federal stuff we're not privy to."

Declan washed the newspaper ink from his hands. "Simone isn't the only one who thinks something's up. Stephanie came by the shop and told me to tell Charlotte to tell *Frank* there's a serial killer in town."

Seamus knit his ample brows. "*Stephanie* did? Why? What's her connection to all of this?"

"She says she has a client who asked her to share the message, but she wouldn't tell me who it was. She didn't want to tell the police herself—supposedly to protect her client. She's hoping Charlotte and Frank can provide her with information in exchange for info she can share."

"Why does she think you and Frank would do that for her?" Seamus asked, turning to Charlotte.

"That's a good question."

Declan pointed to Charlotte and then himself. "That's the thing; she says *we're* somehow involved with these murders or with her client. By working with her, she says we're protecting ourselves."

"Ourselves?" asked Charlotte. "You left out that little tidbit on the phone! What could *we* have to do with any of this?"

Declan shook his head. "I don't know. But things are never straightforward with Stephanie. She refused to explain."

Seamus pulled at his chin. "Hm. This is all very mysterious."

Charlotte smirked. "Seems I'm back on the clock. I'll log my time working on this with you *and* Frank. I'll have all my hours by Christmas!"

"Aye, do," said Seamus. "Help me crack this case and I'll give you a Christmas bonus as well. Simone's got deep, government pockets."

"You don't have to pay me."

"Take it," said Declan. "You may never hear him offer to part with money again."

She laughed. "Fine. Deal." She walked to Seamus and thrust out her hand.

Seamus eyed her outstretched palm. "Should I spit in my hand first? Maybe we should cut our palms and co-mingle our blood?"

"You're disgusting," said Declan.

"I think the shake will be just fine," said Charlotte.

CHAPTER NINE

Declan was packing a set of dinner plates in a combination of foam and newspaper when Stephanie stopped by the shop again.

"Oh, thank goodness you're *here*," she said as the bell announced her arrival. "I stopped by yesterday and you'd been replaced by Chiclets embedded in a blob of saddle leather."

Declan sighed. He knew what she meant. Blade was missing a tooth to the left of his front teeth and one lower incisor. The remaining incredibly white teeth, offset by his Florida perma-tan, made for a jarring juxtaposition.

"*Helloooo*," she said, arriving at the counter and snapping in the air to get his attention.

He looked up from his box of china. "I know you didn't just *snap* at me."

She squinted one eye at him. "*Whatever*. So, who was the old dude? Did someone pawn him?"

"That was Blade. I hired him to watch the store so I could have a day off once in a while."

"Seriously? I mean, I'd understand if you were a dentist and needed a walking-breathing *before* photo, but—"

He rose from his kneeling position. "Yeah,

well...turns out people aren't lining up around the block to sit in a pawnshop all day."

"Just people named *Blade*. Shocker. So what do you have for me?"

"What are you talking about?"

"Any news on the serial killings? Do the cop or *ponytail* know anything?"

"I told *Charlotte* you thought there was a serial killer in town."

"Did you tell her *I* was the one who asked you?"

"Yes. I'm not going to lie to her. Anyway, it's not like you told me who your client is."

"No. So what did she say?"

"Turns out they *did* recently investigate a suspicious death. Two, actually. Frank told Char the Puzzle Killer might be back."

"Really?" said Stephanie, a strange smile creeping across her lips.

"You've heard of him?"

"I have. Growing up here he was like a myth. A boogieman. Go to sleep or the Puzzle Killer will get you, that sort of thing. I remember going to a sleepover and leaving a puzzle piece on a girl's pillow to scare her. Don't you remember him in the news?"

"I guess I preferred to hang with less awful friends. Ones who didn't try and scare me to death."

Stephanie smirked. "What made Frank think it was him?"

"He said the poisoning had all the hallmarks."

"Poisoning? What poisoning?"

Declan grimaced. "I'm not sure I'm supposed to

say. It's information they didn't share with the press."

Stephanie put her hands on her hips. "That's the whole point of this arrangement. Look, don't make this harder than it has to be. I'm trying to help you and Little Miss Legs-a-lot. *Tell me what you know.*"

Declan scowled. "I need some information from you, too. You still haven't explained how *we're* involved. If there's a serial killer after us, isn't that something you should share?"

"I told you; it's just complicated. Client privilege stuff. You're safe *if you tell me.*"

He put his tape gun on the counter. "Fine. For the poisoning, there was a string on the victim's coffee pot. When he pulled out the pot, it released a trap door on the back of the fridge that dumped poison into his milk."

Stephanie crossed her arms against her chest and tilted her head to the side. "How bizarre."

"I thought so, but apparently this is how he works."

"Why didn't I hear about this? I would have remembered all this coffee pot nonsense."

"They left the details out of the paper."

"Was there a puzzle piece at the scene?"

Declan had begun to straighten his counter top, but jerked his attention back to Stephanie. "How did you know? They found a puzzle piece in the butter bin."

She grinned and he scowled.

"Shoot. Not telling you that part was making me feel better about spilling the rest of my guts."

"Anything else?"

"Well sure, you know everything already, why not? There were two other murders."

Stephanie straightened. "What? Two more Puzzle Killer murders?"

"No—I mean, maybe, if they are all related...we don't know. A crossword puzzle champion and a guy eaten by an alligator. They're both accidental deaths that might be murders."

Stephanie's expression took on the strange amused look he'd seen earlier.

"I read about the alligator," she said, her expression returning to its usual unreadable blank canvas. "Who's the crossword man?"

"I don't know his name. Apparently, he fell out of bed and stabbed himself in the neck. But Seamus isn't convinced it was an accident."

"Seamus? Your uncle? How does he know about this?"

"He's been hired by someone to find out if there's a connection between those two murders and any others."

"Who?"

"I don't know her. A woman named Simone. She's with the Federal Marshals. She sent a whole bunch of WitSec people here, so she's worried those people could be involved."

Stephanie ran her hand through her hair. "Interesting..." she mumbled, though Declan didn't get the impression she was talking to him. Her mind was wandering, and he found that comforting. When she was actively thinking about *him*, that's when he had to worry.

"You've done really well," she said, her attention drawing back to him.

"Did that help? Are we safe? Are we done?"

She placed her hand on top of his. "Keep up the good work. I'll see you soon."

He jerked away his hand and she smiled. She held his gaze for a moment and then left. As the door closed behind her, he released his breath. He reached into his pocket to retrieve his cell phone and called Charlotte.

"I delivered the news to Stephanie," he said when she answered.

"Good. Could you glean anything?"

"Something's up. She's playing a game for sure, but I don't get the impression it *really* has anything to do with us."

The bell rang again and he looked up to see the new hire enter.

"Blade is here, I have to go."

"Wait, *who?*" Charlotte said as he hung up.

Declan had to prepare for the second shift. He didn't keep the store open late as a rule—most of Charity's residents didn't stay up very late—but now that he had Blade he thought he'd experiment with staying open until nine. Blade didn't mind. He called himself a *night owl*, which coming from Blade's mouth sounded disturbing at best.

"Hi, Blade." Declan looked at his watch as Blade entered. Third day on the job and the guy was ten minutes late.

Blade nodded and smiled the closed-lip version of his smile. Declan had thought there couldn't be anything more disturbing than Blade's day-glow gnashers grinning at him until he saw the new version of his grin.

"Greetings, Dek-a-lin."

Whenever Blade said *Declan* it sounded like *Dek-a-lin*. Between that and his habit of saying *greetings* instead of *hi* or *hello* he sounded like a pod-person from planet X masquerading as a human.

I hired an alien. I know it.

"It's *Declan*. Like *DECK-lin*."

Blade lifted one side of his upper lip. Declan couldn't tell if it was another version of his smile or an impromptu Elvis impersonation.

"That's what I said, boss."

Declan sighed and put his hands in his pockets. "Sooo...that nickname...*Blade*...where'd you get that, anyway?"

"It's not a nickname. It's my *name*, man. Like the *grass*."

"Oh? Huh. I thought maybe you were good with knives or something." Declan laughed, picked up a pillow and pretended to stab it. Blade stared at him, expressionless. Declan realized how strange he must look and put down the pillow. He fluffed it.

"Sorry. I'm sure it has nothing to do with real knives."

Blade grunted.

Was that a "yes it has nothing to do with knives" grunt

or a "wielding a knife is like breathing to me" grunt?

Declan swallowed. "So you *are* good with knives?"

Blade shrugged.

Humble. Nice. I like knife wielding maniacs modest.

"That...that's quite a coincidence, huh? That your name is Blade and you're good with a...er...blade?"

Why can't I stop talking?

"Not a coincidence. If your name was Milkshake, don't you think you'd like milkshakes?"

"I guess. But you said it was *Blade* like *blades of grass.*"

Blade stuck his tongue in and out through the spot a tooth once lived, and shrugged.

Declan nodded. "Right. Okaaay. So, anything you need before I go? Got the hang of everything so far?"

Blade nodded. "Everything is warmer than a cow's udders."

Declan squinted at him. "I don't even know what that means."

Blade didn't elaborate.

"Okay then, I'm going to go."

Blade pointed at him with his thumb raised and then dipped his thumb, as if shooting a little handgun at him.

Declan clapped his hands together. "*That* is unsettling. Alrighty. On that note, this is me going."

Declan grabbed his laptop and left, thinking it might be a good idea to employ an undercover shopper to check in; maybe the moment he left the shop Blade was dressing roadkill like his dead mother or something. *Had Blade met Seamus yet?* Maybe his uncle could pop by and check if Blade was making sock puppets from the intestines of his customers—

There was a loud crack. Declan ducked and jumped at the same time. He bobbled his computer and remained crouching in the parking lot, his laptop held in front of his face like a shield, his heart racing.

What the heck was that?

He looked around and saw nothing out of the ordinary. He decided it had to be a car backfire.

He straightened, the hand not gripping his computer over his heart.

"What was that?" said a voice. It was Blade, his head poking from the door of the shop.

"I don't know," said Declan. "It scared the heck out of me, though. I guess a car backfire?"

Blade shook his head. "Nope. That was a gun shot."

Declan scowled. "How do you know?"

Blade chuckled and slipped back inside.

Declan stared where Blade's head had appeared and chewed on his lip.

"What have I done?" he muttered.

CHAPTER TEN

Darla, Charlotte's neighbor and Frank's wife, opened her door to find Charlotte on her porch.

"Didn't you say you were thinking about getting a cat?" asked Charlotte.

"Well hello to you too, sweet pea, whatcha'll doin' here? Come in." She did everything but *pull* Charlotte into her home. "Now what's this about a cat?"

Charlotte allowed herself to be ushered into the kitchen. "I thought I remembered you talking about getting a cat."

"I've talked about it. Since our little Oscar died it hasn't been the same. But I don't know if Frank is ready to swap the dog for a cat."

Charlotte paused in a moment of silence to Oscar's memory. Darla's little terrier had passed away a week earlier at the age of fifteen.

"I can confirm he's *not* ready to swap a dog for a cat," said Frank from the kitchen table.

"What are you doing home at ten in the morning?" asked Charlotte.

Frank lifted his coffee mug. The side said *Classy, Sassy & a Bit Smartassy* in a fat black font. "Had an early call. Thought I'd come home and sneak a cup of joe before I went back in."

Charlotte pulled out a chair and sat next to him. "I'm glad you're here. I've got some information for you."

"Oh yeah? What's that?"

"Seamus has a client who thinks the alligator in the pool and the death of that crossword guy about a month back are related. We're wondering if the refrigerator poisoning is connected as well."

Frank scowled. "*Seamus*," he muttered. Frank hadn't warmed to Seamus since discovering he'd been a snitch for the Miami police. *Especially* since Declan's rapscallion uncle had *also* represented himself as a retired cop upon first returning to Charity. Frank found that particularly offensive. Charlotte knew his fib had been to protect Declan's opinion of him. It might not have been right, but it was understandable.

Charlotte decided to pretend she couldn't hear the disapproval in Frank's voice and continued. "Were you called to either of those deaths?"

"Old fella at the Future Horizons retirement home fell on his pen and bled out before anyone found him. *Roger* something was his name. In the *Guinness Book of World Records* for doing crossword puzzles from what I heard."

"So you think he fell on his pen?"

"It was his crossword-solving pen. From what they said, he never let it out of his sight. No reason to suspect foul play. He fell out of bed with it in his hand and stabbed himself in the jugular."

"Yikes."

"Remind me not to carry anything sharp after the age of seventy," said Darla, pulling out a chair to join them.

"You're safe carrying around that brain of yours then," said Frank, winking at Charlotte.

Darla rolled her eyes.

"What if the pen and the alligator weren't accidents? Could they be related to the poisoning?"

Frank shrugged. "I don't know. I don't think anyone was really looking for anything odd about the crossword puzzle guy's death. The alligator death was weird enough on its own. But now that you mention it...there *were* puzzle pieces at the pool. Didn't mean much to me at the time—I mean, the guy made *puzzles*—but now..."

"So they are related! What about the crossword guy? Any puzzle pieces?"

"I don't know. I only heard about it, wasn't involved. Who's this client of Seamus'?"

"A woman named Simone. She's a Federal Marshal from what I understand."

"A Marshal?" Frank made a grunting noise that Charlotte knew was his way of showing his respect. "If I get a little time I'll double check things."

Charlotte nodded, her mind still searching for a connection between the three deaths.

"So what was all this about a cat?" asked Darla.

Charlotte returned her focus to the present. "Oh. I have to go pick up the cat we found at the poisoning. Seems you can't just take an animal to a vet and then leave it there, no matter how noble your intentions. They sorta want you to pay the bill and take it away."

"You're kidding—they said *you* have to pay for it? It isn't even your cat!"

"But I brought it there. It isn't *that* odd that they might think I should be responsible for its bills. Anyway, I'm hoping the dead guy's heirs will pay for it in the end. Hopefully they'll want their parents' cat."

"I figured that cat was a goner," said Frank, finishing his coffee in one gulp and standing.

"Nope. He's a fighter and I thought maybe Darla would like to go with me to get him."

"Well, sure, honey, I'd love to keep you company—"

"*We're not getting a cat,*" said Frank, cutting her short as he hiked up his belt.

Darla shook her head. "No, no, of course not. I'm just going to keep her company—"

Frank held up his hands. "I swear, Darla, if I come home and there's a cat in this house—"

Darla fluttered her fingers in the air. "Don't get yourself into a tizzy."

Frank paused long enough to offer his wife one last squint before leaving.

Darla smiled at Charlotte as the door clicked shut.

"Let's go get that cat."

*   *   *

Charlotte walked into the veterinary's office with Darla on her heels.

"I'm here to pick up a cat," she said to the woman behind the counter.

"Name?"

"Me or the cat?"

"Either."

"I don't know the cat's name. I'm Charlotte Morgan. I found it."

The woman typed on her keyboard and beside her, a printer sprung to life. She ripped the sheet from it and handed it to Charlotte. "Cash or credit card?"

Charlotte looked at the bill. "Two hundred and fifty dollars?"

The woman remained silent.

She sighed and pulled her credit card from her pocket. The woman ran it.

"I'll be right back!"

Charlotte wandered from the counter and sat next to Darla, who had found herself a perch next to a man with a large iguana on his lap.

"Isn't that thing ugly? Why would anyone want a pet without fur?" Darla said to her.

The iguana's owner's eyes shifted in her direction and he frowned.

"I have a point," she mumbled.

He looked away.

A woman in a white coat holding a bald cat walked through the closed bottom half of the Dutch door separating the waiting room from the back offices.

"He's good as new," said the vet, presenting the furless creature, its pink skin wrinkling like a bag beneath her grasp.

"Sweet mother of pearl!" said Darla, her hand rising to cover her open mouth. "Is that some kinda mole person?"

Charlotte reached out and took the cat from the vet and, to her great relief, the cat didn't seem to mind. It crawled up her chest and peered over her shoulder at Darla.

"Thank you," she said.

"You can go back to feeding him his regular food," said the vet, pulling her buzzing phone from her pocket.

Charlotte shook her head. "No, that's just it! I don't *know* his regular food. I—"

Before she could finish her sentence, the vet had already offered a quick wave goodbye and started back toward the Dutch door, her phone at her ear.

Charlotte turned to Darla. "Want a cat?"

Darla grimaced. "Sweety, that isn't a cat. That's an anorexic pig."

"Aw come on, he's *cute*." Charlotte held the cat away from her and peered at it. It looked like it had satellite dishes for ears. "Well, he's probably hypo-allergenic, anyway. That's a plus, huh?"

"Charlotte, if I took that thing home, Frank would poison *me*." She peered into the cat's face. "It does have kind eyes though."

There was a scream from the back and everyone in the waiting room turned their heads in time to see a tiny, brown dog shoot through the Dutch door left ajar by the busy vet during her retreat. A long-bodied puppy nearly tripped on his ears as he slid on his hip during a tight and totally unnecessary loop. He whizzed to Darla's feet and jumped up on her shin, attaching himself like a lamprey.

"Turbo!" screamed a girl, stumbling around the corner after the dog.

Darla reached down and picked up the pup.

"Toy dachshund?" she asked as the dog tried to wriggle up her shoulder and on to her head.

The girl nodded, out of breath from the chase. "Someone abandoned him. Realtor found him in a home. Probably didn't eat for a week. Now we can't keep the little escape artist in one place."

Darla's expression melted into a puddle of love as the wriggling hot dog tried to climb her face.

"Is he still sick?" asked Darla.

"No. He was barely alive when the real estate guy brought him here, but that was weeks ago."

"What's going to happen to him?"

The girl shrugged. "I don't know. I guess if we can't find someone to adopt him, he'll go to a shelter."

Darla's head swiveled toward Charlotte and a familiar smile curled on her lips.

Charlotte's head dropped. "I know that look."

"What?" said Darla, wrestling the dog back into her arms. "Frank said not to bring home a *cat*..."

CHAPTER ELEVEN

"What have you discovered?" asked the blonde woman sitting on the opposite side of Stephanie's desk, her crisp ivory suit barely puckering at the crease of her lap. She held out a bottle filled with caramel-colored liquid. "Oh, and I brought you a gift. Open and pour."

"Bourbon? It's ten o'clock in the morning."

"And your point is—?"

Stephanie looked at the bottle. "Pappy VanWinkle? Isn't this thousands of dollars?"

"If you were to buy it, yes."

Stephanie opened the bourbon, sneaking peeks at her most troublesome client, Jamie Moriarty, as she prepared to pour. She admired Jamie's suit, and her sapphire earrings, encircled by tiny pearls. The woman had style.

The woman also claimed to be the Puzzle Killer. Stephanie wasn't entirely sure she believed her.

"I like your earrings," she said.

"Thank you. Now what do you know?"

"Well, there was one more suspicious murder. A couple poisoned. Atropine was dropped into their *own* milk after they unknowingly triggered a simple machine. Sound familiar?"

Jamie jumped in her chair. "They *did* find it! The paper never mentioned the machine—"

"It was *you*? You poisoned them?"

"It was my *answer* to the other murders. I was trying to get his attention. Let him know he's not so special. I never dreamed the papers wouldn't mention *how* they were poisoned."

"A string tied to a coffee pot? Really? That seems so..*bourgeois* for the Puzzle Killer."

The woman rolled her eyes. "It was spur of the moment. I didn't want to put a ton of effort into it. But hey, don't I get extra points for killing *two* people?"

"I suppose. I don't know how the serial killer point system works."

"You definitely get extra points for killing a couple."

"Great. Let me ask you this: If you did it...was anything left at the scene?"

"I left a puzzle piece in the dairy box on the door of the refrigerator. They never mentioned that either." She shook her head. "What's the point of killing people to get someone's attention if they don't put all the details in the press?"

Stephanie grimaced. Jamie had the puzzle piece location correct. *Maybe she really was the Puzzle Killer.* She felt a rush of adrenalin. *Talk about a high profile case.*

"Why *that* couple?" she asked. "Are they significant?"

Jamie shrugged. "The woman cut me off in

traffic. Sometimes I act out of civic duty."

Stephanie sighed. "So our mystery man kills a crossword puzzle champion and a puzzle maker to get your attention, and you respond with an act of road rage."

"And thanks to the press, he never received my message."

"You two are like some kind of deadly rom-com, full of missed chances and misunderstandings. Maybe you should just meet him on top of the Empire State Building like *Sleepless in Seattle* and kill all the other tourists together."

"Very funny. You mean *An Affair to Remember*. *Sleepless* was a knock-off. Yeesh, young people are annoying. Think they know *everything*."

Stephanie scowled. "Look; all fun aside, keeping secrets isn't going to make my job any easier."

"Oh *please*. Representing me is a lawyer's dream. You're loving every minute of this."

"No—"

Yes.

"No. Believe it or not, defense lawyers generally prefer *innocent* clients."

"Please, you're as wrapped up in this as I am. He contacted you to be a go between. He's got *your* number, too." Jamie offered a mirthless smile and stared past Stephanie through the office window. She refocused with a little gasp, as if she'd remembered something. "I meant to ask...do you think this *Declan* is an asset?"

Stephanie straightened. "Yes. It doesn't hurt to

have someone on the inside. His"—she turned her head and pretended to spit on the ground—"his *girlfriend*, Charlotte, knew about the fridge poisoning, and while I know now that wasn't quite the *news* I thought it would be, we don't have Charlotte and her sheriff buddy without Declan."

Jamie hummed and Stephanie cocked her head.

"Wait. Why are you asking me about Declan?"

"I was going to help save you from yourself, but as it happens, what you just said occurred to *me* in the nick of time last night."

"What does *that* mean?"

"I thought maybe I'd give you a little present."

Stephanie slapped both her hands on the desk. *"What does that mean?"*

Jamie waved her hand dismissively. "Don't worry. I didn't kill him."

"Why does that sound like it is about to be followed by a *but?*"

The woman smirked. "Well, I might have sent a shot across his bow, so to speak."

"How so?"

"With a gun. I sent an *actual* shot across his bow."

"You *shot* at him? That seems a little uncomplicated for you, doesn't it?"

Jamie laughed. "You should know the Puzzle Killer is a very small portion of my work. I do maybe one puzzle killing a year just to keep the legend alive."

Stephanie tilted back her head before training a

steely gaze on the woman across from her. "*Do not kill Declan.* He's *mine.*"

"That's what I'm afraid of. Why him? What does he have you could *possibly* need?"

Stephanie felt her jaw tightening. "I don't see how that is any of your business."

"Fine. What about Charlotte? Can I kill her?"

"No. She's our direct line to the sheriff. Oh, *and* Seamus, Declan's uncle. He's looking into the puzzle murders, too. Detective, hired by someone called *Simone*, could be important. Do you know a Simone?"

Jamie shook her head. "Maybe she's a reporter."

"No, apparently she's a Federal Marshal. Does that catch your attention?"

"It does."

"Good. So you can see Declan and Charlotte need to stay alive if we're going to keep our edge."

Jamie flicked her wrist in the air. "*Fine.* I won't kill her until we're done."

Stephanie slapped the desk again. "Don't kill Charlotte *ever*! If you kill her, you'll turn her into a martyr. Declan will be pining for her for months until some sweet empty-headed little thing finds a way to console him."

"Couldn't *you* be that sweet, empty-headed little thing?"

"*Ha.* Just leave them both alone. I need him to come to his senses on his own."

"On his own?"

"Maybe not *entirely* on his own. But let *me* handle

things."

Jamie shook her head. "What you see in him anyway."

"If you must know, he's the sweetest person I've ever known."

The woman lifted her gaze toward the ceiling. "Exactly. How boring."

"He's also incredibly handsome."

"I'll give you that. But there's something deeper here, isn't there? I just can't put my finger on it—"

Stephanie grimaced. "How about we get back to you and your multitude of problems."

"I thought we covered all the new news?"

"All the news by way of Charlotte and Declan, but I have other news."

"Oh? What's that?"

"An email."

"An email?"

"From your admirer. Nothing you can trace. I had my people try. It's bouncing from IP to IP, probably originating somewhere in Pakistan."

"This guy is in Pakistan?"

"No, his email server is based there."

Jamie huffed. "Speak *English*."

"I have his email address. You can't use it to trace him or find where he is, but you *can* use it to talk to him."

"Really? How did you get it?"

"The delivery method followed his usual modus operandi. Originally, he put that ad in the paper telling "PK" to contact me and by some miracle, you saw it and figured out it was a message to the Puzzle Killer, right?"

Jamie ran her tongue across her teeth. "I wouldn't call it a *miracle*. I'm not an idiot."

"I mean it's a miracle he guessed your general location and that you actually read the paper that day."

Jamie shrugged. "I'll give you that."

"He was less subtle with me. Left a note about the people he murdered for you on my doorstep. He wanted us to talk without you two discovering each other's identities."

"Yes."

"Then we thought he went dark. But he didn't. Not really."

"What do you mean?"

"I went back and looked at the press coverage of the alligator attack. Did you see the picture in the newspaper of the pool?"

"Yes."

"Did you notice on the lounger there was a newspaper open to the personals? There was also a flashlight sitting next to it and a glove with the fingers folded to point to it. He couldn't have tried harder to make you notice it if he'd draped it in Christmas lights."

"There were? I couldn't stop staring at the puzzle pieces floating in the water..."

Stephanie opened her desk drawer and retrieved a newspaper. Slapping it on the desk, she pointed to the photo under the headline "Alligator Attacks

Puzzle King." It depicted a backyard pool surrounded by EMTs and police.

Jamie squinted at it. "My eyes aren't what they used to be."

"I saw the glove and thought, *why is there a winter glove there?* See the pattern on it? It's little snowmen."

"So both the glove and the flashlight are pointing to the paper? I told you, I don't have my glasses with me."

"*Yes.* So I put a cryptic ad in the personals telling him we were awaiting further word. Shortly after, he—and one random nut job who saw the ad—sent me an email."

"Did you—"

"*Yes.* I checked. It was untraceable."

"So how do you know it's *this* person who's been killing people to get my attention? Couldn't anyone have responded to the ad?"

"Yes. But I'm sure this the right person."

"Why?"

"The email was AlexGator@erectionpillz.com."

Jamie's lip curled. "Alex? Is that his name?"

"I suppose."

"And did you say *erection pills*? *That* tells you he's the right guy? Honey, you have a lot to learn—"

"*He's using a spam server for his email.* The important part is the *gator*. No one but the real killer would know my ad had anything to do with the alligator killing."

Jamie sighed. "You know who I should have killed? The guy who invented the Internet."

Stephanie wrote the email down on a piece of lined yellow paper, tore it from the pad, and handed it to her client.

"Don't use it yet. I'm going to get you an email account so you can talk to him. Untraceable."

The woman stood and took the paper. "I hate all this. I don't know why I'm giving this idiot the time of day."

"Because the idiot is *here*. Your home turf. He's closer than you think to figuring out who you are. He didn't send you to me on *accident*."

"Oh, right. Good point." She walked to the door and then turned. "Hey, how's Debbie?"

Stephanie scowled. "You mean the woman you left me with so you could run around the country killing people?"

She nodded. "That one."

"She's dead."

"Oh." Jamie shrugged. "That explains why I haven't heard from her in a while. She was a useful lady."

Stephanie nodded. "She did her best."

"Well, thank you for all your help."

"My pleasure, Jamie."

Jamie paused in the doorway. "Can you call me the *other* name? I think I'd like that."

Stephanie sighed.

"Fine. It was my pleasure...*Mom*."

Jamie smiled. "See? Wasn't that nice? Have you enjoyed our time together?"

"Sure. I'm *over the moon* that it took another

murderer threatening you to bring you to me."

"But I *told* you. I told you I was your real mother. Don't I get points for that?"

"You told me...only after I told *you* the packet I received from the killer *said* you were my mother. And only after you paid me so the information would fall under attorney-client privilege. Which, since I received that information independently, technically isn't covered, FYI."

"*Still.* I could have denied it."

"You could have. And it would have been crushing *not* to find out my mother is the Puzzle Killer."

Jamie grinned. "Oh come on. It's kind of *exciting*, isn't it? I mean, I am *famous!*"

Stephanie stood and walked to her mother. She took her hand in her own.

"What are you doing?" asked Jamie, trying to tug back her hand.

Stephanie held it tight and watched as the intimacy of their connection made her mother's eyes ring white with fear.

"Mother, I need to ask you something."

Jamie paled. "What's that?"

Stephanie stared into her mother's eyes. "If this guy kills you..."

Jamie scoffed. "He *won't.*"

Stephanie nodded. "I know. But if he does?"

Jamie tried jerking away her hand again but Stephanie held on. "If he does, *what?*"

"If he does—can I have those earrings?"

CHAPTER TWELVE

Jamie had been so many things during her illustrious career as a serial killer. She'd begun at seventeen, murdering her own drug-addicted mother by overdosing her while she was wrapped in a heroin dream. Her mother had done most of the work with her own needle; Jamie only finished the job. Her mother'd had cancer, so it hardly even counted as murder. She told herself it was a mercy killing, before realizing she didn't *need* justification.

She didn't care.

Her mother's death served as a gateway drug of its own. Jamie's initial success killing her mother made it easier to punish her *father* for *leaving* her mother. He, and the cancer, had been responsible for pushing her mother into the depression that led to her heroin addiction in the first place.

Daddy's death took some planning. Living with her agreeable but uninterested aunt, Jamie plotted for nearly a year. She knew killing him too soon or too obviously would arouse suspicion. Eventually, eleven months after her mother's death, she called her father and begged him to let her visit him at his new home in Orlando. He agreed to pick her up, though he made it clear the prime motivator for his kindness was free babysitting for his new son. He and his new wife wanted to take a cruise to the Bahamas.

He arrived on time, and Jamie hopped into his truck, a bowl of potato salad like her mother used to make cradled in her arms. She told him it was a gift for his kindness. He barely looked at the food. Or her.

He certainly didn't see the glued crack down the center of the bowl.

Jamie buckled in, and, once they reached a decent speed, jerked her father's steering wheel, sending the truck into a tree.

She'd underestimated the force of a pre-planned car accident. She broke her nose on the dash. Poor, unlucky Daddy caught a shard of the glass potato salad bowl she'd brought in the neck and bled out before the ambulance arrived.

The fact that the *stabby* part occurred sometime after the crash was an inconsequential detail.

With very little effort, the bowl had split along the crack Jamie created the day before. A crack she'd glued together with cheap white glue. She knew a *knife* in her father's neck would be difficult to explain, but a shard of glass from a potato salad bowl during a car accident? *That was just bad luck.* No reason to give it another thought.

Even then, as a fledgling killer, her murders had a sense of *poetry*. Back when Jamie's mother discovered her father's cheating, she'd thrown a bowl of potato salad at him. It was one of Jamie's most vivid childhood memories; potato salad exploding against a wall.

Mom missed.

She did not.

In both cases, potato salad was *everywhere*.

Jamie left her aunt's home soon after the crash. She murdered strange men for the contents of their wallets for years before developing the Puzzle Killer persona. Murder had become too easy and she'd wanted to put a *twist* on her exploits. A little *flair*.

She was smart, and that helped her avoid the authorities. More importantly, she was gorgeous, and being beautiful was ninety percent of the battle when it came to setting a man-trap.

At first her puzzle murders were simple; not puzzles at all, really. A man cheating on his wife with a ravishing young drifter might open a hotel door tied to the trigger of a shotgun, for example. It thrilled her to kill people *and* make the deed their fault. Not because it removed her guilt, but because it made them as culpable as she. Her victims were her accomplices.

It made things less lonely.

But she quickly tired of the shotgun-string trick. Even if the victim technically caused his own death, it was obvious *someone* set the crude trap. The situation lacked finesse.

She moved on to murders that looked like terrible accidents. That saved the trouble of the police looking into their deaths. Then, emboldened by her success, she created elaborate traps and began leaving puzzle pieces at the scene. She'd wanted to leave potato salad as an homage to her beginnings, but it proved too impractical.

Once, she wired a cat box to a trigger switch. A woman in a store had bumped into her while lifting a bag of cat litter into her cart. She didn't even say excuse me. Jamie followed her home. The next day, she broke in and found the cat box. Then she found the cat. She weighed both and went home, where she built a switch that would set off an explosion if the weight of the cat box was ever more than ten ounces over the weight of a clean cat box, litter and the cat. She figured ten ounce of cat poop was too much to forgive.

It took six days for the bomb to blow. Could be the cat gained weight, or maybe there was a second cat she'd missed, or the woman pushed on the box...but Jamie liked to imagine the trigger was laziness. People should clean cat boxes more often.

It wasn't that she was particularly fond of cats; a few weeks earlier she'd paid a man to teach her how to set up mercury switch bomb. So *someone* was going to blow for *something*. She had to practice her new skills. She was a firm believer in learning by doing. And that cat ladies should have had better manners.

In addition to the fact she was always learning, the key to Jamie's longevity as a serial killer was simple. Since killing her parents, she'd never dispatched anyone she *knew*. Without motive, most investigations fizzled.

She didn't need to know her victims. Strangers could annoy her in an infinite number of ways.

She also never *told* anyone. It baffled her why so many murderers blabbed to strangers, lovers and bartenders. It reminded her of a Benjamin Franklin quote she'd heard in grade school.

Three can keep a secret, if two of them are dead.

Following those two simple rules kept her free and alive, apart from *two* exceptions. First, her husband. That was necessary evil; it's hard to be a killer *and* keep a full time job. She needed a lifetime of money. So she'd chosen him partly for his trust fund but, more specifically, for the decade long feud he'd had with his brother. When the two of them killed each other during an argument with no witnesses other than the dead brothers themselves, there was little reason for the police to suspect *her*.

But though no one blamed her, she did have one growing problem.

She was pregnant.

Though it would take over twenty years, the pregnancy lead to her second exception.

She left the child, Stephanie, with a sympathetic, baby-desperate childhood friend back in Charity, Florida, shortly after giving birth. No one knew about Stephanie. Unwilling to share custody with her husband's family, Jamie gave away the child before anyone ever knew she existed.

She'd done right by the girl. Paid for her college and law school. Kept her adoptive mother in food, clothing, beer and shelter. Now she had a lawyer built into her family.

How convenient.

Who knew you could just *make* a lawyer.

But she'd broken her second rule by sharing information with Stephanie. When this *Alex* person sent Stephanie a package stating Jamie was her mother *and* the Puzzle Killer, she could have denied it all, but she didn't. Thank goodness for lawyer-client privilege. Stephanie had taken the news like a trooper. Finding out your new client is a famous serial killer *and* your mother might have destroyed lesser women. She respected the girl for her composure.

Jamie sat at her kitchen table in front of the laptop computer Stephanie had set up for her. She turned it on. It worried her that the person trying to catch her attention had killed the crossword champion by making it look as if he had fallen on his own pen. Both the *death by accident* and the sweet irony of the weapon being his own beloved puzzle pen was *her* style when she *wasn't* the Puzzle Killer. Did this annoying killer-wanna-be *know* that? Or did he just get lucky? It was one thing for him to obsess over her carefully-crafted public persona as the Puzzle Killer; it was another if he also knew most of work went unnoticed, with no one knowing they were murders at all.

She suspected this fan of hers was young. No established serial killer would waste his time proving his devotion to an idol. Putting her poster on his wall, so to speak.

Jamie opened the email account Stephanie had

set up and watched the wheel turn as something downloaded.

I've got mail.

The subject line said: *First time emailer, long-time fan.*

She opened it and read. The body of the email only had one sentence.

Do I have the honor of talking to the Puzzle Killer?

She typed back: *Who wants to know?*

It sounded juvenile, but it was an important question.

The response came back almost immediately, announced by the ring of her email notification.

Bing! Just call me Alex. I don't have a cute nickname. No one knows about me. I'm that good.

She grimaced. *What a little snot.*

What do you want, Alex? she typed.

Bing! Your tally.

Was that some sort of slang the kids were using now?

My what?

Bing! How many victims. I want to know your tally of victims.

The emails were coming and going so quickly Jamie felt as if the man was outside her window. As if they were connected. It was unsettling. *Who was this?*

Bing! You probably think you're the most prolific serial killer of all time, but not for long. I imagine you'll never tell me your tally, so I propose this: Let's have a contest.

Jamie scoffed, both at the notion of a murdering

contest and the idea that this idiot had killed more people than she had.

Why would I do that?

Bing! If you don't, I'll reveal your identity to the police.

Jamie's fingers hovered over the keys for a moment before typing. She felt rising anger.

You're bluffing.

Bing! Am I, Jamie?

She gasped. She hadn't used her given name with anyone other than her daughter in nearly forty years. She stared at the screen for so long that another email arrived.

Bing! Need some time? You can pick the game. You have two days.

She typed four letters.

Time.

She hit send, shut off the computer and sat, stunned. Then she stood, picked up the laptop, and dashed it to the ground.

CHAPTER THIRTEEN

"I'm just glad it doesn't have claws," said Charlotte.

Darla, Mariska and Carolina had stopped by to usher her to water aerobics. They hadn't been in her home for more than two seconds before they'd burst into giggles, but she couldn't blame them. She had an eight pound naked cat wrapped around her neck. The Sphinx she'd inherited from the poisoning case was terrified of her terrier. She couldn't move without it wrapping itself around her neck like the world's ugliest furless stole.

"How can you move with that thing around your neck?" asked Darla.

"I make do. He's terrified of Abby-dog and the poor thing has already been through enough. Lost his mommy and daddy."

"Why don't you lock Abby in the bedroom?" suggested Carolina, petting the cat.

"Why should my dog have to be locked in a room just because an uninvited guest is scared of her?"

"That *doesn't* seem fair," agreed Mariska.

Charlotte reached up and scratched the cat behind his ears. "When he's actually around my neck it's easier to leave him there, because when he's not, he's hopping from place to place trying to get high enough for a running leap at my head. The first day he made a wild jump from the kitchen counter and attached himself to my face like one of those creepy-crawlies from *Alien*."

The women continued to cackle.

"Poor thing," said Charlotte, petting the Sphinx's face, which was pressed against her cheek. She could feel his body rumbling with a low purr. It wasn't unpleasant; maybe cat neck massages would be the new rage. "I feel bad for him. It won't be the end of the world if I have to wear him for a day."

"What happens in a day?' asked Carolina.

"The poisoning victim's kids are coming to close up their parents' house and I can drop him off. I was finally able to reach them and let them know I had him."

"Oh, that's good. What a terrible thing they must be going through, losing both parents in a matter of days."

Charlotte nodded, walked to the bedroom and pulled the cat from her shoulders to plop him on the bed. The cat spun and tried to make a leap at her, but she was ready for it. She dodged, ran out of the room and shut the door.

"You look like you've done that before," said Mariska.

Charlotte smiled. "Guilty as charged."

"That's how I used to get away from my children," said Darla.

On their way out, Abby ran up the hallway and positioned herself on her stomach, nose pressed against the crack at the bottom of the bedroom door, snuffling.

"That poor cat is going to have a nervous breakdown," said Carolina, peering down the hall at the curious dog. "How'd you'd like to be locked in a room with a monster sniffing outside the door?"

"Reminds me of my ex-husband," said Mariska.

Darla slapped her arm, laughing. "You're terrible."

Charlotte led the ladies out of the house. "If poisoning didn't kill him, I don't think a little stress will."

"Oh!" Darla touched her arm as they walked down the driveway. "Frank told me to tell you that they found puzzle pieces next to the crossword guy, whatever that means."

"It means the few deaths we've been investigating are probably related and probably murders," said Charlotte, mulling over the news. She realized she was smiling and Darla was staring at her.

Darla rolled her eyes. "You people are a bunch of sickos."

The four of them took Mariska's golf cart to the community pool. Darla gave Carolina her usual seat beside Mariska and perched on the rumble seat beside Charlotte. As Mariska screeched around the corner, Charlotte had to grab Darla to keep her from tumbling off. In the process, she accidentally slapped

Darla's left breast.

"Oh, I'm sorry!" said Charlotte. "I was just trying to keep you from falling!"

"No problem," said Darla. "That was the best sex I've had in years."

Charlotte grimaced and laughed.

"Mariska!" Carolina's knuckles were white, holding the rail beside her seat.

"What?"

"Slow down! You drive like a crazy person!"

Mariska pulled into the parking space beside the pool.

"You're all a bunch of wimps," she said, gathering her towel and foam floating noodle.

They waved to Jackie, Seamus' girlfriend, as she set up the boom box for blasting the water aerobics cassette tape. Things were always the *highest* tech in Pineapple Port.

Struggling to disrobe from their cover-ups, Charlotte was the first to spot the smooth operator making his way toward them. It was Lester, the same tiny, tanned man who'd attempted to proposition Carolina at lunch in St. Pete Beach.

"You're right, he *is* from here," said Charlotte, tapping Mariska's arm and nodding towards the approaching man.

Mariska followed her motion and spotted Carolina's admirer. "Oh boy, this should be good," she muttered to Charlotte. "He wants a pussy cat but he's going to get a tiger."

"Hello ladies!" said Lester, holding his hands in

the air as if he'd just completed a marathon. "Look at you!"

Charlotte watched as Carolina's eyes squinted into tiny slits.

"Trying a little aerobics today?" he asked, winking at Carolina.

"No, we thought we'd try the horseback riding," she said. "But it looks like only the backend has shown up."

Darla tittered.

The man plowed ahead as if he hadn't heard her.

"I think we might have gotten off on the wrong foot—"

"My feet are just fine," said Carolina, and she walked into the pool without another word.

"Excuse my sister," said Mariska. "She's a married woman and she doesn't like any nonsense. Are you new in town?"

His gaze lingered on Carolina a moment longer and then he turned his attention to Mariska. "I am. Just moved here a couple of months ago. I'm renting the Tilladays' house."

"Oh?"

He nodded. "Have some business in the area."

"What sort of business are you in?"

Before Lester could answer, the music blared to life.

"We better get going," said Darla, pulling on Mariska's arm. She caught Charlotte's eye and whispered, "She'd talk to a tree stump if we let her."

"Don't I know it," said Charlotte.

With a tight smile she offered Lester a nod and entered the pool with the others.

The ladies lined up and began swinging their legs to the music.

"Charlotte, I've been meaning to talk to you," said Jackie, taking a spot beside her.

"What's up?"

"I'd like to hire you."

"Hire me? Why? Your boyfriend is a private eye. Just tell *Seamus* to get on the case."

"Well that's just it—Seamus is the reason I need you. I want you to follow *him*."

Charlotte stopped swaying to the beat. "*Follow* him? You think he's cheating on you?"

"Something's up. I can tell. I went through all of this with my husband and I am *not* getting caught off guard again."

Charlotte sighed. "I don't know, Jackie. I don't feel great about following him. He's kind of my boss. And he's definitely my boyfriend's uncle—"

"I know. I'm putting you in an awkward position. I'm sorry. Maybe you could just keep an eye out when you're around him? Generally?"

Charlotte thought about Seamus' new client. *Simone.* Maybe Jackie had caught him talking to her and confused her for a girlfriend. She shrugged and nodded. "I suppose it wouldn't hurt to keep my eyes open. Unless I find something, of course. That *would* hurt."

"Yes, it would," said Jackie, her expression

souring.

"Charlotte, did you hear about the plants?" said a voice from the opposite side of the pool.

She turned to see Penny Sambrooke wading towards her. She and her husband George owned Pineapple Port.

"Hi Penny, it's good to see you," said Charlotte. Penny was about as friendly as a shrew with heartburn, but she'd been having some marriage problems lately. Charlotte thought it would be nice to give her the benefit of the doubt before bracing herself for the worst.

"I said, did you hear about the plants," Penny repeated, in a sharper tone.

So much for kinder-gentler Penny.

"What plants are those?"

"Someone has been stealing plants from all the houses in Pineapple Port."

"All the houses?"

"Well, not *yours*. You never bother to plant any."

Charlotte winced. "They always die—"

"Someone's stealing plants?" said Mariska, moving toward the conversation in a slow, half-dancing, half-walking pace. "I thought an animal dug up my sunflower!"

"I'm missing some marigolds," said Darla. "Well, I'll be. I just figured Frank found them dead and tossed them in the bin."

"What kind of neighborhood is this?" said Carolina aloud to no one in particular. "People stealing plants, Lester the Molester lurking about—"

Mariska laughed and the two of them began to giggle. Penny shot them both an evil glare.

"Penny, tell me what you know," said Charlotte, trying to distract her from the Cackle Twins. She didn't want to see a war between Penny and Carolina. With that many sharp tongues flying around no one at water aerobics would survive.

"Someone's stealing plants," said Penny, turning her sharp glare back to Charlotte. I don't know how else to say it."

"So, they're taking a few plants from each house?"

"Exactly."

"At night?"

Penny scowled. "If I knew *when* they were stealing things, *I* could catch them. That's *your* job."

"*My* job?" Charlotte cocked an eyebrow. "Am I on the Pineapple Port payroll now?"

"Catch him and we'll talk," said Penny, turning and tossing her hand into the air to be sure Charlotte knew she'd been officially dismissed.

Charlotte looked at Mariska. "Nice to see *she's* back."

Carolina lifted her nose and hand in the air, imitating Penny. "La te da."

CHAPTER FOURTEEN

Jamie watched Charlotte and her dog stroll down Pineapple Port's neighborhood street. Now was her chance. She'd slip inside and look around. See if there were any skeletons in Charlotte's closet and get a feel for the layout of her home, just in case. Anyone involved in your life, in any capacity, was worth having leverage against. If Charlotte was involved in Stephanie's life, she needed to be vetted.

And who knew? Jamie didn't like the idea of Stephanie devoting herself to a slice of white bread like Declan, but maybe clearing the path to love for her daughter would allow the silliness to run its course. She'd come to her senses and move on.

Of course, Stephanie said she wasn't *allowed* to kill Charlotte, but maybe she could make the girl less *attractive* to Declan. Maybe a little *accident*. Charlotte might lose a leg...maybe a disfiguring fire...

She sighed. Best not to start making plans. For now, spying on Stephanie's rival would keep her mind off Alex, her homicidal fan. She still had to decide how to handle *that* situation and she didn't want to think about it.

Her phone rang.

She grimaced. She hated cell phones. She should

have left hers at home. The little squawk boxes were too unpredictable.

"Hello?"

Stephanie began talking without the usual pleasantries. "I got your message. Why did you say the computer I gave you is in pieces all over your floor?"

"Because I *threw* it to the floor." Jamie looked up and caught a glimpse of Charlotte disappearing around the corner.

"*Why*? Where are you? Are you at home? Tell me where you live and I'll bring you another, but—"

Jamie bit her lip. Stephanie was angry about the computer, but she would be *furious* if she knew she was anywhere near Charlotte.

"I'm food shopping."

"Look, we need to talk about this situation. Did you talk to the killer?"

"Yes."

"Well, what did he say?"

"He's confirmed his name is Alex."

"Do you know him?"

"Look, this will have to wait. I have errands to run after this. A hair appointment—"

"I thought you were food shopping."

"I am."

"You're going food shopping and *then* running errands all day?"

"I'm not getting frozen goods. Just, uh...cans of things and whatnot."

Jamie dropped her head into her hand. *How could*

she be such a terrible liar when it came to such mundane things? Maybe she'd been alone too long. She'd forgotten how to talk to normal people about normal things.

"So you're out *specifically* shopping for canned goods?" asked Stephanie. "Are you building a bomb shelter?"

"No, look, I'll talk to you later. Make an appointment. Pick a time."

Jamie hung up the phone and turned it off. She had to get moving if she was going to have any time in Charlotte's house before she returned. She'd timed the girl's walk during the previous day's surveillance. Charlotte circled the neighborhood three times, and it took her twenty minutes for each revolution. She still had time to get inside before the girl finished her first loop.

Jamie hopped out of her car and strode to Charlotte's unlocked door. Slipping inside, she made a quick scan of the depressing mediocrity within. The wall leading into the kitchen had been painted with chalkboard paint. On it, was a food shopping list and a list marked *Cases*. Scrawled beneath that heading was *Catch Puzzle Killer?*

Jamie smiled.

Good luck with that.

She moved down the hall to the bedroom. The door was cracked open. If the girl had anything to hide, it would be in there. A person's bedroom always belied their true nature.

Jamie entered and yelped before slapping her

hand across her mouth. A small, dark-haired man with skin the color of nutmeg echoed her surprised squeak and scrambled out of Charlotte's bed. As he stood, a pair of women's underwear slid from his chest to the floor.

"What are you doing here?" he asked in a heavy Latino accent.

She looked to her side and spotted what was obviously Charlotte's open underwear drawer. She squinted one eye at the man.

"Shouldn't I be asking *you* that?"

He held up his hands. "It's not what it looks like."

"It *looks* like you're lying in Charlotte's bed with her underwear on your chest."

"What? Where?" he looked down and slapped his chest. "There is no underwears. You are crazy. I am here to fix the pipes."

Jamie scowled. "I think you are here hoping to *clean* her pipes, creep."

The man's eyes assumed the glazed look of someone not listening and his hips shifted slightly. Jamie could tell he was concentrating on pushing the dropped panties under the bed with his foot. She chuckled silently at his ridiculous plight and pondered her decision. *Kill him or let him go?* He'd seen her face, but he couldn't tell anyone about her without incriminating himself. *Still,* she didn't like lose ends. *Or creeps.*

She sized him up. Physically he wasn't large and even in her fifties, she reckoned she could take him.

He'd be caught off guard by her strength, skill and determination. But even a little wrestling would make a mess. Charlotte would know someone had been in her house and DNA would be littered all over the room. And while no one would do a DNA test on a tossed room after an apparent break-in, if for some reason Charlotte later went *missing*... No. Too risky.

"I'm Charlotte's aunt. I want you out of here right now!" she demanded, making her eyes blaze with what she hoped looked like angry indignation.

He nodded and held up his hands. "Yes, yes. I go. No problem. I...I fix the pipes later."

She stepped aside and let him hurry past her, resisting the urge to hook his throat with her forearm. She walked to the bedside and plucked the pair of pink panties from the ground, folded them and placed them back in the drawer.

She returned to the kitchen and paused to give the house one last visual sweep. Time to abort today's mission. It hadn't been a successful visit but, on the upside, she hadn't had time to make any mistakes. Still, she liked to think a moment before she left a room to be sure she didn't leave anything behind, or miss a detail that could cause her trouble down the road.

A shuffling noise caught her attention and she felt something hit her back, high, near her shoulder. She grunted and whirled, expecting to find the Peeping Tomas. Nothing was behind her but the kitchen island, but she could still feel *skin* against her neck, a weight, as if someone had dropped a sack of flour, wrapped in warm soft leather, around her neck.

She scrambled to reach behind her head, clawing at her ears and shoulders. As her fingernails dug into the object, it yelped, and she felt a pinch on her hand. The weight released from her shoulders and she heard something hit the floor behind her. She turned in time to see a pink creature scurrying down the hallway to the bedroom.

What in the name of hell spawn was that? She rubbed at her neck, hoping she hadn't already been contaminated by whatever infected that pink, baggy-skinned attacker.

Jamie put her hand on her chest and took a moment to catch her breath. Remembering the painful pinch on her hand, she studied the red mark there. It wasn't deep or bleeding in any significant way.

She peeked around the corner and saw two green eyes staring at her from beneath the bed at the end of the hall.

Cat.

Killing the cat would reveal her presence in the house.

Right?

Yes.

"Lucky cat," she hissed at it.

It stared.

She slipped out of the home and into her car without extracting her revenge.

As she pulled away, in her rearview mirror, she could see Charlotte rounding the corner for home.

Between the peeper and the leper cat, it was a miracle she'd escaped alive.

Jamie rolled past the Pineapple Port grounds-keeping building and spotted a familiar man there, stacking plants on the back of a flatbed golf cart.

Her old friend, Peeps.

Charlotte's admirer was a grounds keeper for the community. He was someone who saw her every day and knew when she walked the dog; knew when her house would be empty. That made sense.

She felt a familiar tingling in her blood.

Peeps posed a threat to Charlotte. Stephanie didn't want Charlotte dead, fearing her martyrdom would only delay any chance of her regaining Declan's love. Using that logic...

It would be irresponsible of me not to protect Charlotte, wouldn't it?

And forget Charlotte; *Peeps had seen her.*

She hated loose ends.

And creeps.

"This should kill an afternoon," she mumbled, pulling to the curb and readying herself for a day of surveillance.

CHAPTER FIFTEEN

Charlotte had just stepped out of the shower when she heard a knock. Abby burst from her post-walk nap and ran for the door. Charlotte slipped on a robe to follow.

Outside, she found Auntie Carolina.

"Are you taking the cat back today?" she asked.

Charlotte nodded. "I was just getting dressed. Come in."

Carolina stepped into the house and immediately spotted the cat on the refrigerator.

"You go ahead and get dressed," she said, heading for the kitchen.

Charlotte nodded and padded back to her bedroom. Once dressed, she returned to the living room to find Carolina on her sofa with the cat wrapped around her neck.

"He doesn't make me sneeze," she said.

"Are you allergic to cats?"

"I had one as a girl and my mother had to give it away because of my allergies. This guy doesn't make me sneeze."

"He seems to like you—oh shoot."

"What's wrong?"

"I was going to borrow a cat carrier from Declan's shop and I totally forgot to ask him about it."

"I'll go with you," offered Carolina. "I can hold the cat."

Charlotte nodded. "Okay, great! We're taking Mariska's car."

Carolina pulled the cat from her neck and into her arms to carry it outside. Charlotte heard the creature's happy purr engine rumbling as the two passed her.

They borrowed Mariska's car and headed to the scene of the poisoning. The son had told Charlotte he would be there all day packing and she could bring the cat back any time. He'd also promised to reimburse her for the vet bill.

"Are you going home?" said Carolina in a baby voice to the cat, who had rolled onto its back in her lap like a dog searching for a belly rub.

"He's a real dog-cat," said Charlotte. "Looks like a cat, acts like a goofy dog."

"I'm not sure he even looks like a cat," said Carolina, before shifting back into baby talk. "You're a little weirdo, aren't you? Aren't you?"

Charlotte pulled up to 745 Locust Lane. All the blinds were closed. It didn't look like anyone was there.

"Wait here a second," said Charlotte, getting out.

She went to the door and knocked, but there was no answer. Peering through the window, she could see the house was empty of furniture.

Oh no. Did she get the day wrong?

"Hello?"

The neighbor next door was on her porch in her housedress calling to her.

"Hello?"

"Hi," said Charlotte. "I was supposed to meet the son of the former owners here today?"

"You heard what happened," said the woman, her voice dripping with drama.

"I did."

"Hey! You were here when they found Rich... You were with the Sheriff?"

"I was."

"You missed Rich Jr. He came with a moving van and took everything yesterday."

"Yesterday!" Charlotte sighed. "I was supposed to meet him and return his parents' cat."

The woman laughed. "Rich Jr. hated that creepy-looking cat. He told me yesterday he wished it had died too..." she trailed off. The two women looked at each other, reaching the same conclusion at the same time.

"So, he told me to show up a day late because he didn't *want* the cat," said Charlotte.

The woman nodded. "Seems like it."

"I don't suppose *you* want a cat?"

The woman opened her door to head inside, laughing. She shut the door behind her without another word.

"I'll take that for a *no.*"

Charlotte returned to the car.

"Looks like I've got a cat. At least until I can find someone else who wants him," she said, turning the ignition.

"What do you mean?"

"The guy purposely gave me the wrong day so he wouldn't have to take the cat back. He's long gone."

"Oh, that's terrible," said Carolina. She nuzzled the cat's face to her own. "Isn't that terrible Mister Mister? But you get to stay with us...yes you *do*..."

Charlotte glanced at Carolina. She'd never seen this soft and fuzzy side of the woman. Strange the fuzzy side appeared for the least-fuzziest thing on the planet.

Charlotte stopped at Declan's pawnshop on the way back to see if he had a cat carrier. Carolina came into the store with her, cat in her arms.

"Hello there!" said Declan, weaving his way through the furniture maze to greet them when they entered. "What brings me this pleasure today?"

"I've been duped and I need a cat carrier. You mentioned you had one?"

"I do. I'm Declan," he said, thrusting his hand toward Carolina.

"This is Mariska's sister, visiting from Michigan," said Charlotte.

"Nice to meet you," said Declan.

Carolina shook with her non-cat-cradling hand. She was staring at Declan. Charlotte suspected she was trying to find something to *not* like about him.

The absence of wisecracks meant so far, so good.

"Enjoying the weather?" asked Declan. "Little warmer here than Michigan, eh?"

Charlotte silently groaned. Declan had just tossed Carolina a softball.

"Ya think?" said Carolina.

Charlotte braced herself for more, waiting for Carolina to call Declan *Captain Obvious* or tell him he should have been a weatherman—what with him knowing Michigan is colder than Florida and all.

Instead, she *smiled*.

"It's like a darn sauna. The place is only fit for ferns!" she said and then giggled.

Giggled.

"So this is the cat," said Declan, rubbing the creature's head as it pushed its ears against his fingers. "Really neat looking, isn't it?"

"Isn't it?" said Carolina, beaming.

What is going on here? Declan had won over Carolina. Charlotte had never seen her Auntie warm to another human being that quickly. Heck, it had taken four visits before Carolina stopped calling Darla "Hayseed" due to her Southern accent.

"Let me get you that carrier," said Declan. He went to the far left side of the store and came back with a cat carrier, a glittery collar and some toys.

"The collar might be a little girly for him," he said.

"No, it's perfect," said Carolina, snatching it from his fingers.

"What do I owe you?" asked Charlotte.

"Don't worry about it."

"Bye!" Carolina twirled on her heel and headed back to the car.

"I think she's eager to put the collar on him," said Charlotte. "Thanks for everything."

"No problem. So you have a cat now?"

"Looks like it."

"At least it doesn't shed."

Charlotte sighed. "Yeah, I've got that going for me."

CHAPTER SIXTEEN

Jamie preferred to plan her appointments. It was the best way to avoid costly mistakes. She watched the peeping Tom maintenance man for an hour, popped home for a cup of coffee when it was clear he'd be busy working for the foreseeable future, and returned at four p.m.

Peeps was there in the maintenance yard, emptying the flatbed of a golf cart-turned work truck.

Perfect.

Over the next hour, Peeps hosed down the truck, smoked two cigarettes and shared a couple of beers with his co-workers. She noted he was left-handed. Little details like that sometimes came in handy.

At ten to five, the little man disappeared behind the maintenance shed and an old Toyota pickup emerged a few minutes later; Peeps at the wheel.

Jamie followed him home with no plans beyond discovering the location of his residence. She toyed with the idea of Peeps at the center of the game she was supposed to play with Alex. *First one to kill Peeps, wins.* She'd choose him for the game, as if at random, but all the surveillance work would be done.

That's when it hit her; she couldn't have a

murdering contest with mysterious Alex. If she didn't kill the chosen prey first, she lost. But killing first might be the whole point of the game; he could surveil *her*. Watch her planning the murder and watch her committing it. She couldn't assume he didn't already know who she was and where she lived.

Winning was losing. Heck, he could *film her winning.* These days everyone had a camera, ready to quick draw like a gun at a moment's notice. Selfie pout? *Snap!* Well-cooked quinoa? *Snap!* Nailing the infamous Puzzle Killer for murder? *Snap!*

She sighed.

How hard would it be for him to send me to jail or blackmail me for life?

Winning his battle was losing the war.

A wry smile curled on her lips.

She almost respected him for thinking of it.

Bastard.

Well, that answered *that.* There would be no contest. It was ridiculous anyway. She'd have to find another way to appease the nut. On her own terms.

She took a moment to mourn the high-tech, new generation of murders.

They just don't make serial killers the way they used to.

Peeps parked his truck in front of a small cement brick house at the end of an overgrown cul-de-sac. There were no other cars in his driveway, no children's toys littering the yard and no obvious signs of a woman's touch.

Surprise, surprise.

His neighborhood was largely abandoned; both

neighboring houses had *For Sale* signs and the faded blue rancher across the street was boarded.

She felt a tingle of excitement.

He might as well have driven home to a remote camping site. And here she was, Jason Voorhees in his hockey mask, ready to slaughter the lustful teen guidance counselors.

After all, it did turn out to be Mrs. Voorhees who did all the killing in *Friday the 13th*.

Sometimes life just drops things in your lap.

Peeps went inside and she watched him through the curtain-less front window. He grabbed a beer and stationed himself on the sofa in front of a glowing television.

Jamie turned off her engine. Pulling a gauzy scarf from her purse, she wrapped it around her right hand.

Don't do it. It's too tempting; don't do it, said a little voice in the back of her head, but she still found herself opening her car door.

She walked to Peeps' backyard; a small, overgrown affair encircled by a rusting metal fence. A large bush from the neighbor's abandoned yard had engulfed the fence and now commanded a good portion of Peeps' yard. The gate to the fence was open, as was the rotting shed skulking in the far corner. On the ground outside the shed was a baseball. She picked it up.

She peeked inside the shed and spotted a short machete leaning against a wall.

Is someone writing this murder for me?

She had everything she needed. An abandoned neighborhood. A baseball. A machete.

Everything was perfect.

She grasped the machete and tested the weight in her scarf-wrapped hand. It felt good.

She walked to the front of the giant bush at the back of the yard and tucked the baseball under her armpit. Turning to face the house, she rested the machete on the ground by the tip, so the handle balanced on the back of her leg.

She unbuttoned her blouse and pulled it open. She considered removing her bra, but decided it was unnecessary.

Plucking the baseball from under her armpit, she threw it as hard as she could at Peeps' door. There was a loud crash as it struck the aluminum bottom portion and the glass above shattered to the cracked cement steps below.

Knock, knock.

Peeps appeared a moment later, beer in hand. "Que?—"

He opened the broken door and skittered down the stairs before he realized what stood before him. A crazy, half-dressed old—*mature*—lady. He stopped and stared, his jaw hanging open.

Jamie held out her hand and crooked her finger, beckoning to him. Like a man hypnotized, he walked towards her.

I've still got it.

Once or twice he hesitated, but she cupped her breast with her other hand, running her tongue across her lips. She felt like a cartoon. Still, he continued.

Men are such idiots.

When he was about four feet away from her, Jamie opened her palm, transforming her beckoning finger into a stop sign. Like a good boy, he stopped.

"You want me?" she purred. ¿Tu me quieres?

She watched confusion cloud his expression. He didn't know why this was happening. Slowly, his confusion morphed into a sly smirk. She assumed he'd come to the only conclusion a man would; that she'd seen him at Charlotte's house and now she just *had* to have him.

Naturally. Things like that happened all the time to the guys in *Penthouse Letters*, right?

"Step forward with just your right leg," she whispered to him. She tapped her own leg to be sure he understood.

For a flash, the confusion returned to his expression, but then he laughed. He stepped forward with his right leg, so he looked as if he was about to attempt a split. He wobbled and giggled.

"Close your eyes while I unwrap your gift."

Grinning, he closed his eyes.

Jamie had to move fast. People always peeked. Especially Peeps. He'd be the first to peek, wouldn't he? She certainly couldn't trust *him* to keep his eyes shut.

She reached behind her with her wrapped hand, grabbed the handle of the machete resting against her leg and swung it, embedding it deep in his groin. The angle of the wound was almost parallel to the ground, just as it would have been if he'd swung at a giant bush and missed. He was left-handed, after all. He would have hit the inside of his upper *right* thigh.

She pulled the weapon away as quickly as she had swung it, and dropped it to the ground as the blood soaked through his thin jeans.

He opened his mouth to scream and she lunged forward, whipping the scarf from her hand and shoving it into his mouth. She positioned herself behind him, her arms wrapped around his, pinning them to his sides.

Peeps fell back on his butt and she went with him, still holding him tight. He struggled and tried to throw his head back into her face, but she easily avoided it.

A minute later he was still.

Severing a femoral artery had that effect on people.

Jamie pulled her scarf from Peeps' mouth and again wrapped it around her hand. She stood and used the machete to hack wildly at the monstrous bush until she'd made an obvious dent in the plant's progress toward yard domination.

Holding the metal part of the blade, she pressed Peeps' palm and fingers around the handle of the machete and then dropped it to the ground beside him.

She took a step back. As she admired her work, she noticed his beer on the ground next to him.

Nice touch. Good of him to bring it out with him.

How ironic that a landscaping professional like Peeps would fatally wound himself while pruning his own bush, but...when alcohol is involved...*what can you do?*

She re-buttoned her shirt and walked to the backdoor, stopping to retrieve the baseball before heading back to her car with it.

She tossed it and caught it as she walked.

Jamie drove to her storage unit. She rented it after realizing that keeping certain incriminating items in her living space was like sleeping on a bomb. Somewhere she'd picked up the nasty habit of accumulating mementos from her appointments. Not jewelry or clothes or *toes*; just random items from the scene that caught her eye. It fulfilled her urge to keep trophies without making them so important she'd be done in by the collection.

She also kept her getaway case at the unit, filled with fake passports and identities and cash. She left Peeping Tomas' baseball there on the shelf and selected a small bottle of chloroform from a case. She had a feeling she might need it on hand.

She found her leather-bound journal and wrote *Peeps* in it. She'd written notes about all her victims in a book written in a cypher that only she could break. When she was too old to kill, she would send the book and the key to deciphering it to a publisher. Then, she would disappear and wait. Hopefully, she would live long enough to watch the book rocket to the top of the best-seller lists. It was silly, but she thought that would be the closest thing to *reliving* her life.

She'd wanted Jodie Foster to play her in the movie adaptation, but she'd come to realize the actress would be too old by then. One day she'd really have to consider the casting more seriously.

Leaving the storage facility, she noticed a car parked down the street and realized she'd seen it earlier. *Was that Alex? Was he following her?*

She toyed with the idea of confronting him, but decided it wasn't time. She didn't know enough about him yet.

Pretending not to see, she got into her car and headed downtown where it would be easier to lose the tail. When she felt safe, she headed for home.

Parking in her driveway, she pushed her hair from her eyes. *I have to be more careful. I have—*

Jamie's hand brushed across her ear and she realized she was missing an earring.

Oh no.

CHAPTER SEVENTEEN

"Hey," said Declan, setting down his bowling ball. Mariska's husband, Bob, had a bowling team and Charlotte had talked him into filling in for one of the missing members.

That was weeks ago.

Now he was a bowler.

Luckily, when a man owned a pawnshop, it wasn't hard to find a used bowling ball. He unzipped his bag and pulled out the black orb he'd nicknamed *Chuck*. First, because he *chucked* it down the lanes. Second, because it had *Charles Womak* engraved on the side. Declan liked to imagine the real Charles Womak bowled a three hundred, had a heart attack from the shock and died with a smile on his lips.

There were worse ways to go.

Declan stared at his rented bowling shoes, wondering what critters were dying with smiles on their faces in *them*, when he overheard Bob talking to Lester, another new member of the team. Lester had been shuffled into the lineup after Phil threw out his back leaning over to retrieve a cheese fry he'd dropped. No one could say if he'd been planning to eat it off the carpet, but it was the source of much speculation.

"You have to keep *pressing*," said Bob. He sounded very serious.

Lester shook his head. "I dunno. I really get the impression she doesn't like me. And she's married."

"Oh, you don't *know* Carolina," said Bob, waving at him dismissively. "She's *lying* about being married."

"She did have a ring."

"She got it from a Cracker Jack box. You've got her right where you want her."

Lester sighed. "If you say so."

"You'll see. You stick in there. I'll put in a good word." Bob patted him on the shoulder and stood to head toward the concession stand.

Declan strode after him, his feet shifting in the ill-fitting shoes as he went. Much bigger feet had stretched the twelves into thirteens. Lots of feet.

A whole *bunch* of other people's feet.

He shivered.

"Bob," he called, reaching forward to tap Bob on the shoulder. Mariska's husband was a little hard of hearing, which, he said, was why he and Mariska had been married for so long.

Bob glanced over his shoulder.

"Declan! You want me to get you a beer?"

"Sure. Hey, what were you talking about with Lester? Something about Auntie Carolina?"

Bob started chuckling. "What you heard, my boy, is pure *genius*."

Declan flanked him to the beer window and Bob ordered brews by holding up two fingers.

"Tell me," urged Declan while they waited.

Bob began chuckling again, making it difficult for him to speak. "I told him to pursue Carolina."

"Pursue? You mean flirt? Try and date her?"

Bob nodded, holding his stomach. "She's going to *hate* it."

"Carolina *is* married, right?"

"Yep. She hates people flirting, too, but I've got Lester in a froth. He's going to hunt her like a coon hound. She's his little squirrel."

Bob hooted and wiped away a tear of laughter. Declan couldn't help but grin.

"So you're trying to torture her?"

Bob nodded and snorted. The noise took him by surprise and made him laugh harder. "It's no more than she puts me through every time she shows up. The woman can't stand me. I don't know why. But two can play that game."

"Charlotte told me she's a teetotaler. Maybe she just doesn't like the fact you enjoy a fine bourbon once in a while."

"Oh she *hates* drinkers." The server put two mugs of beer on the counter and Bob lifted his into the air.

"Cheers!"

Declan bowled a one hundred sixty-six. It was the best official game he'd had in a while and he was feeling pretty good about the evening. He sat back in his chair to finish the last drop of beer and noticed red and blue lights dancing on the cement wall of the bowling center. While colorful, the lights paled compared to the bowling alley's disco night lights, so he turned to look for the source. He spotted a police cruiser parked outside; sirens off, lights on. Two policemen entered the building, clearly looking for someone.

"Wonder what that's about," he said to no one in particular. Lester was sitting one chair away from him. He was slumped down low, his expression frozen and unreadable. "You feeling okay, Lester?"

"My car. Car trouble. Could you give me a ride back?"

Declan nodded. "Sure. Let me just return these shoes—"

"Bob will do it," said Lester, grabbing Declan's shoes and placing them on top of Bob's. Bob had wandered outside to have a cigar with some of the other men in the league.

"Okay..."

Lester stood and scurried out of the bowling center, giving the cops a wide berth. He exited through the side door, which no one ever used, even though Declan had left through the front.

Confused, Declan continued to his car and Lester appeared shortly afterward, opened the back door of the car, slid in and shut the door.

Declan scowled and looked from Lester to the police car and back again. He opened his own door and sat inside.

"Something you want to tell me, Lester?"

"What's that?"

"Why are you slumped in my back seat?"

"Oh, I'm sorry. I have a little bit of a stomach ache. I knew I shouldn't have had the fried shrimp. If you could maybe hurry?"

Declan's eyes narrowed. Now he didn't know what was worse; having a wanted criminal in his car or having a man about to lose his bowling alley fried shrimp all over the back seat.

He started the engine and pulled out. Pineapple Port was only fifteen minutes away. Chances were pretty good Lester wouldn't throw up *or* kill him in that short a distance.

"Is there anything I can do?" he asked.

"No, no. Just get me home. Thanks. I really appreciate this."

Declan nodded and drove. He was only on the road five minutes before he spotted the flashing lights in his rearview mirror.

The cops had followed him.

"I wasn't speeding," he said.

"What?" Lester sat up like a gopher and peered out the back window. "Did you run a stoplight or something?"

"No."

Declan began to pull over.

"Just keep going," said Lester.

"What?"

"They don't want you. Just keep going."

"Lester, they're right behind me."

The police car released a little *whoop whoop!*

"See? They want *me*."

He pulled over and Lester began to groan.

"Your stomach," said Declan, putting the car in park. "Are you going to be alright?"

"Oh no no no no..."

"There was a tap on the window and Declan rolled it down.

"Hello officer, how can I help you?"

The policeman shined his light on Lester through the back window. "Do you know this man?"

Declan turned and looked at Lester as if he was surprised to find him in the back seat.

Do I know Lester? Who really knows anyone?

He refocused on the officer. "He's Lester. He's in my bowling league. He asked for a ride home."

In the passenger side mirror, Declan could see the officer's partner open the back door. He asked Lester to step out. Declan squinted at the image.

Does he have his gun drawn?

Lester slid out of the car, looking very small and worried, his hands held aloft.

"Wait here," said the first cop.

Declan waited and watched as the officers walked Lester to the curb and began questioning him. He tried to inch down the passenger side window, but with the traffic going by, he couldn't make out the conversation.

Oh Lester. What did you do?

He gasped, remembering his conversation with Bob. *And who was Bob sending after Carolina?*

Five minutes later the police officer was back at Declan's window.

"You can go," he said.

"What about Lester?"

"He's coming with us." The officer lingered to see if Declan had a problem with that.

No problem.

He rolled up the window and drove home.

The rest of the drive he could only think about one thing: Charlotte was going to be *so* disappointed in him when he couldn't tell her why the police took Lester.

CHAPTER EIGHTEEN

During her morning dog walk, Charlotte noted missing plants in many of the front yards around Pineapple Port. Someone was definitely helping themselves to the landscaping. She was a little disappointed she hadn't noticed *before* Penny pointed out the thefts. Seamus would have been horrified at her observational skills.

A rectangular piece of paper had lodged itself in the blades of grass of Darla's front yard and she picked it out, recognizing it as one of the doorknocker advertisements that showed up from time to time. A few doors down she saw another resting against the side of a painted cement alligator, and she grabbed that one as well. It was a door hanger for a power washing service. There had been a bit of a squall the night before; the wind had blown the hangers from their doorknobs. She hadn't seen one on her own door, so one of the offending pieces of trash was probably hers. She looked on the back. In pen was scrawled *Zeke P.* She reasoned Zeke P. received a bonus for any leads he generated.

Zeke P. would do better if he checked the weather.

Staring at the advert, Charlotte had a thought. Zeke P. saw every house in the neighborhood and visited each briefly before scurrying away. Some of the residents were easily enraged by things like people spamming their doors, so he probably did it at night or very early in the morning before anyone would see him.

And if no one saw him, couldn't he help himself to their plants?

No.

It couldn't be that easy, could it?

Companies hired young people to do these sorts of jobs. Why would a kid want to steal plants? And why would he steal plants and then leave his signature at every crime site?

Still...

Wrapping Abby's leash around her wrist, Charlotte pulled her phone from her pocket, flipped over the door hanger and called the power washing company.

"Is Zeke there?" she asked.

"Zeke?" The man sounded confused. They probably hired an outside firm to do their door hanging.

This would be a dead end. *Serves me right for thinking it could be this easy.*

"Zeke doesn't come in for another half an hour."

Ha! Door-hanger-Zeke did work for them! They couldn't have *two* people named Zeke.

"Oh. Half an hour? He said something about selling his car to me."

"His truck? Really? He loves that thing."

"The black Chevy, right?"

"What? No. Zeke's got an old white Bronco. Lady, I think you have the wrong guy."

"This is Pete's garage, right?"

"No this is Pete's Power Washing."

"Oh! I'm *so* sorry."

"No problem."

Charlotte hung up. She held her breath a moment, hoping the man wouldn't find it odd that there was a guy named Zeke at fictional Pete's Garage, too. She was afraid he'd call her back to explore his suspicions.

She walked another block with no phone call.

Heh.

Zeke would be in in half an hour.

Charlotte returned home, showered and changed while Abby wandered to her bowl for a drink.

Something felt different.

She watched the dog for a minute, and then realized the thing she felt amiss was Abby's daily bolt around the house after her walk. Today, there was no frantic gallop from room to room. Just as suddenly as the tradition began, it had stopped.

She hoped she wasn't going to have to take Abby to doggy therapy.

Pete's Power Washing was only fifteen minutes away. Her hunch was probably nothing, but a lead was a lead, and she intended to follow up on it. If she could solve the case of the plant-nappings, maybe Penny would send all sorts of little jobs her way. The

Case of the Clogged Recreation Center Toilet. The Mysterious Appearance of the *Ensure* Nutrition Shake Bottle in the Pool. The possibilities were endless.

She passed her fridge and ducked, allowing the cat to sail over her head onto the island.

Nice try.

She shut the door and headed for Mariska's. She was nearly there when she saw Mariska at the window. Charlotte pointed to the car and then herself and Mariska nodded. She could borrow it. The keys, she knew, were on the floor.

Charlotte didn't even have to slow down to scan the parking lot as she neared Pete's Power Washing. An old white Bronco matching Zeke's boss' description was parked on the street outside the small brick building. She noted the license plate and drove another block before parking.

She had two options. She could sit, watch and hope Zeke went home for lunch, or she could call Frank and beg him to run the license for her. Pineapple Port was his neighborhood, after all, and plants were disappearing at an alarming rate. That meant a lot of irate neighbors. Why *wouldn't* he look up the license plate for her?

She called the Sheriff's office and the new receptionist, Ruby, answered.

"Hey Miss Ruby, it's Charlotte. Is Frank there?"

"Well, *hello to you*, you sweet thing! You know, he is *not*. Out and about. Wanderin'. He's a wanderer, that one. Hates sittin' at his desk. Can't get him to do no paperwork, no how."

"Oh." Charlotte sighed. Things had been going too well on this case, it was silly of her to think *everything* would fall into place.

"Whatcha need, baby?"

"I was hoping he could run a plate for me. I have a lead on a rash of plant thefts."

Ruby hooted with laughter. "Look at you. Such a little *detective*. Lot better-lookin' than the mess we have around here, too, let me tell you."

"Well, thank you. I guess I'll—"

"Now hold on, I'll run that plate for you. Just give me a minute to get to the other room."

"You?" Charlotte heard the phone hit the desk and then nothing for several minutes. Finally, Ruby's melodious voice returned.

"Sorry 'bout that. Got caught up with Deputy Dippity there for a second. Now what's the plate, sugar?"

"Can you do that? Are you sure? Won't you get in trouble?"

"Aw, you don't worry about me. I do this all the time. I looked up the car parked at my neighbor's house the other day just to confirm she was havin' an affair. And she is. With her boss, too. *Shameful.*"

"Okay. I guess I shouldn't look a gift horse in the mouth."

"Who you callin' a horse?" Ruby cackled with laughter.

Charlotte rattled off the license plate of the white Bronco and Ruby relayed Zeke's address.

"Thank you so much, Ruby. This was *much* easier

than sitting here watching this guy all day to find out where he lives," said Charlotte.

"Well, baby girl, way I see it I owe you one."

"How do you figure?"

"Frank's been tickled pink since you started working with him. And the better mood he's in, the better off I am."

Charlotte laughed. "I'll keep trying to make him happy for you."

"I appreciate that."

Charlotte checked her rearview to be sure Zeke's truck was still parked and then headed for his home. Her brow furrowed as she pulled into the Sturdy Oaks retirement community. She'd pictured Zeke much younger than the fifty-five-year-old requirement age.

Double checking the map app on her phone, she rolled down Bark Street looking for number two hundred twenty-four.

As soon as she saw the address given to her by Ruby, she knew there'd been no reason to creep down the street for fear of missing it. The house looked like a garden center had thrown up on it. Flowers covered every inch of the front yard.

She parked Mariska's car a few houses away and hopped out to give the property a more thorough inspection on foot. She was nearly to it when she spotted a woman in a lavender turban sitting on the screened front porch. She froze, but the woman looked up and locked eyes with her. Turning and walking back to the car wasn't an option without appearing suspicious.

"Quite a garden you have," she said.

Even through the screen, she could see the woman break into a brilliant smile.

"Isn't it wonderful?" The woman rose from her chair and opened the screen door to poke out her head.

With the number of flowers littering the yard Charlotte knew she had to have the right address, but as long as she was talking to the woman, she figured she might as well poke around about Zeke. The woman definitely wasn't the plant-napper, she was fragile and moving slowly.

"Did you do this yourself?" she asked.

The woman shook her head. "Oh no, no. I couldn't do anything like this. It was my grandson, Zeke."

Bingo. Charlotte smiled, her mystery solved. "He must be quite a green thumb," she said, planning her retreat.

"He did it as a present for me," said the woman, stepping out onto her step. She wore a baggy, flowered house dress over a bony frame. "I have cancer. He thought it would cheer me up. I don't know where he got the time or the money, but it makes my day every day to see it."

Charlotte surveyed the garden. It really was beautiful. The eclectic nature of the plants he'd been able to steal made the arrangement seem all the more magical, unplanned and beautiful in its chaos. Still, thievery couldn't go unpunished.

The woman continued, cutting short her thoughts. "Every day there's a new flower. We play a game where I have to guess the new addition." She chuckled. "I swear, I think the only reason I keep living is to guess the new flower each day."

Oh for the love of—

Zeke's grandmother beamed as she admired it from her step, and Charlotte knew she could never tell Penny that she'd found the flower-napper.

She sighed. Thievery *would* go unpunished.

Yea, thievery. Yea, Zeke.

"Well, it's beautiful," she said.

"Thank you."

Charlotte waved and continued to walk, planning to circle the block to return to her car so the woman didn't think it was odd of her to about-face and head back the way she'd come.

That was okay. She was in a good mood.

"Yea, Zeke P," she mumbled, slipping out her phone. She dialed.

"Pete's Power Washing," said a voice, younger than the man she'd spoken to earlier that day.

"Could I speak to Zeke?"

"This is Zeke."

"Zeke, I was just talking to your grandmother."

"Uh...okay...who is this?"

"How do you think your grandmother would take the news that all her flowers were stolen from other neighborhoods?"

The phone went silent.

"I'm not going to tell her, Zeke. Not if you do

two things for me."

"What?"

"First, no more stealing from Pineapple Port."

"Okay."

"And I'd like a power washing. My house. Tell them *Zeke P.* sent me." She winked.

"You want it free?"

Charlotte huffed, disappointed that the meaning of her cool wink had been missed by the boy. "No, not *free*. I'm getting you a commission. You get credit when people respond to our flyers, right?"

"Yeah."

"So put me down for one power washing."

"Okay...but you just caught me stealing—"

"I think what you did for your grandmother is sweet. Just don't steal from my neighborhood."

Zeke offered a nervous chuckle. "Deal."

Charlotte gave him her details and hopped back in the car.

Case solved.

CHAPTER NINETEEN

Jamie returned from a visit to her daughter's law office, more careful than usual to be sure no one followed her home.

She plugged in her new, *new* computer. After she'd smashed the last one in a fit of pique over the intrusion of the upstart copycat killer, Stephanie had been kind enough to supply her with another. Now there was nothing left to keep her from responding to Alex's ultimatum. There would be no game to prove who was the better predator. They would have to come to another solution.

All this showboating. How could she explain to this murderous idiot that she didn't care about her score card?

No, that was a lie. She cared. She just felt confident her numbers were unrivaled.

She turned on the computer and found an email awaiting her.

Have you chosen a game? - Alex

She sighed.

This was ridiculous. She typed.

Leave me alone.

She stood to leave, but stopped at the sound of an email notification.

Bing! We'll pick one person. Whoever kills that person first, wins.

Jamie rolled her eyes.

No.

Bing! Then you pick the game.

No.

There was a pause, and for a moment, Jamie thought she'd ended it. Then, the cursed *Bing!* of new mail rang out.

I have a better idea. I'll pick someone for you to kill. I'll give you a week. If you do it, I'll leave you alone. I promise. Forever.

She decided it was time to confess to Alex that she'd guessed his plan to trick her into committing a murder so that he could witness it. Time to stop the nonsense.

I can't murder anyone for you. I won't. Even if I wanted to, you could be a cop for all I know. Or you could film me killing him or her. This is a ridiculous setup.

Another pause. At least she had him thinking.

Bing! Would a cop have this?

Below his comments was a list of very familiar names.

A list of everyone she'd killed going all the way back to her mother.

How was this possible?

Her journal.

Alex must have stolen the journal she kept in her storage unit *and* solved the cypher, unlocking all her secrets. Revealing all her murders.

She screamed.

Bing! This list is going to the police if you don't kill the person I choose.

She typed *Why? Why are you doing this?* hit send, and left her hands hovering over the keyboard, shaking with fury.

Bing! Yours is not to question why. Or how. But you can see there will be no question about the veracity of any report I make to the police.

Jamie took a moment to calm herself. This wasn't the time to panic. She had to be very careful. She licked her lips and typed. *You know who I am. You know what I'm capable of.*

Bing! I do. Your journal made for fine reading. Enlightening.

Then you know I will find you and kill you.

Bing! Like this?

There was a file attached to the latest email; an MP3 file. She didn't know what that meant, but she clicked on it. A movie began to play, and she watched herself slice Peeps with the machete. It looped, she chopped, Peeps bled. Over and over.

Alex knew who she was. He'd stolen her journal. He'd been following her for, who knew how long?

She looked out her window. *Did he know where she lived?* She was always so careful not to return home until certain she wasn't being tailed. Still...she'd forgotten to be careful leaving Peeps' house and led Alex straight to her precious storage unit.

Jamie let her fingers dance over the keys for a minute. Whoever this was, he didn't talk like a cop. If he was police, he wouldn't have filmed the murder and she'd already been in jail. *How could she have been so stupid?* How did she not see someone watching her?

The movie of Peeps' murder was icing on the giant slice of humiliation cake Alex had already served.

He had enough evidence to put her away for life, and he'd *already* been in a position to kill her. If he wanted her dead, she'd be lying beside Peeps.

Maybe it wouldn't hurt to kill *one* person and make him go away. Maybe that really was all he wanted.

She wouldn't go away though.

She would hunt Alex down and kill him.

Jamie closed the looping murder scene and returned her attention to the keyboard.

So if I kill someone for you, you'll leave me alone?

Bing! Yes. A specific person.

Who?

There was a longer delay than usual.

Bing! Stephanie.

Jamie felt the blood drain from her face. Of course. Alex knew Stephanie was her daughter. She nearly typed *Stephanie who?* but there was no point in playing dumb. They both knew.

Bing! Deal?

She sat straight in her chair and typed four letters.

Deal.

CHAPTER TWENTY

Stephanie watched the screen as an email popped into her inbox. It was her mother's message from the very special computer Stephanie had set up for her. It was her mother's last email to Alex.

Deal.

Stephanie read the word several times and then closed her laptop.

My mother is going to kill me to save her skin.

She picked up her phone and dialed her mother. "Hello?"

"Hey *Mom*, how's the new computer? You didn't already break it, did you?"

Stephanie could hear the saccharine in her mother's nervous chuckle.

"No. Of course I didn't break it."

"Did you talk to him?"

"I did."

"What did he say?"

"Nothing. He's...he's nobody. He won't be bothering us anymore."

"Really? How do you know?"

"I just know."

"But Mom, he killed two people just to get your

attention, don't you think you need to take him seriously?"

"I took care of it."

There was a pause. "Should I ask how?"

"I wouldn't."

Stephanie sighed. "Okay."

"I'll talk to you more about it later. I'm in the middle of something."

"Okay. Well, tell me if you need anything."

"I will. Oh, hey, Steph, where are you now? Staying in Debbie's house? Or do you have a place of your own? I never thought to ask. Maybe we should have dinner and discuss things—"

"I'm..." Stephanie paused. Giving Jamie any more information was like driving to her and laying out her neck for slicing. Not to mention, old *Mom* hadn't told her where she lived either. Hadn't had her over for pot roast.

She decided to play it cool. "I'm here and there."

"Ah, okay. Are you going to be at the office tomorrow?"

"Sure. Maybe. I've got to go."

Stephanie heard her mother trying to catch her, but she hung up. She stood and gathered everything from the office that she thought she would need.

It wouldn't be safe to come back to the office for a while.

It wouldn't safe to go home either.

She smiled.

This gave her an idea.

CHAPTER TWENTY-ONE

Declan heard his doorbell and fumbled in his haste to finish lighting the candles.

"Just use your key!" he called.

He had a romantic dinner planned for Charlotte and, as usual, she was a little early. He cursed himself for not allowing more time to prepare the meal after work, but Blade-the-new-hire had shown up wearing a tie-dye t-shirt with a giant marijuana leaf on it, and he'd had to wait while he went home to change. Blade claimed he thought the image was a maple leaf because he'd bought it in Canada. The idea that a t-shirt, with or without a marijuana leaf, wasn't appropriate work wear, hadn't occurred to him.

The doorbell chimed a second time.

"Coming!" *Maybe she was carrying things and had her arms full.* The last time she'd shown up with an entire corn casserole compliments of Mariska. She claimed if she hadn't brought it, *she* would have eaten the whole thing by morning. Instead the two of them ate it by the end of the evening.

He jogged to the door and flung it open. "You're early—"

Stephanie stood on his doorstep. She had a suitcase in one hand and her eyes were pink and puffy. Her eyeliner remained unsmudged.

"What are *you* doing here?" he asked.

"I need your help," she said, pushing past him into the house.

He glanced out the front door for whatever trouble might be following her, turned to follow her, and bumped into her. She hadn't gone far. She'd dropped her suitcase and flung both arms around his neck before he'd realized what happened.

"Declan," she sobbed. He felt hot tears against his neck. He held his arms out straight on either side of her, worried that if he embraced her she'd stick to him like napalm. Her left hand remained around his neck but her right slid down and began stroking his chest.

"Calm down," he said, peeling her away. "Ouch!" He slapped his hand over his chest. "Did you just pinch my nipple?"

Her expression registered deep indignation. "No! How could you think I'd do that?"

He rubbed his pec. "Right. What's wrong *now*?"

Her forehead crinkled and her lower lip quivered. "It's the most horrible thing that could ever happen."

"*What* is?"

She put her hand over her mouth, her eyes flowing with tears.

No, no. Not falling for this again.

"Stephanie, I've got things to do. Either tell me what's going on or get out of here and give your tears back to the crocodile you stole them from." He nodded to her suitcase. "Otherwise, you'll be late for your reservations at the Witch Carlton."

She burst into sobs and stumbled forward, tripping on her suitcase. As he caught her she again wrapped herself around him like a boa constrictor. Her legs had turned into noodles, incapable of supporting her weight, so he stood there, weighing the pros and cons of dropping her.

That's when the front door flung open.

"I brought wine!" said Charlotte, holding aloft a bottle as she worked to remove her key from the door with the other hand. She looked up and froze.

Declan lowered Stephanie until she had to support her own weight or drop to the floor like a ragdoll.

"Charlotte, you remember Stephanie," he said.

"Uh, *hi*," said Charlotte, closing the door behind her.

"Stephanie here is wildly upset about something, but she hasn't yet found the way to tell me *what*."

The strap of Stephanie's silk camisole slid from her shoulder, revealing enough of her breast to imply she was either braless, or the proud owner of the world's tiniest bustier. With a coy glance at Charlotte, she righted it.

"I'm sorry to hear this," said Charlotte, slapping the wine on the counter a little more loudly than usual. She leaned against the island. "Please, don't let me stop you from sharing."

Stephanie's eyes grew wide and doe-like. "Could I have a glass of wine? It might help calm my nerves."

Declan looked past Stephanie to watch Charlotte's eyes narrow. She caught his gaze and, rolling her eyes, shrugged one shoulder as if to say, *whatever.*

"I've got it," said Charlotte. She opened the kitchen drawer and pulled out a corkscrew.

"Here, I'm sorry; I'm being *so* rude," said Stephanie, walking over to take the bottle from Charlotte. "Let me do it. I know how his screw works—"

"Oh *come* on!" said Charlotte, jerking back the bottle. "That didn't even make sense!"

Stephanie held up her hands. "Oh! Oh, what did I say? I didn't mean it *that* way," said Stephanie, sniffing as she carefully wiped the tears from her eyes with the tip of her middle finger. "Sorry. Really. Honest." She put her hand on Charlotte's arm and Declan could see that if Charlotte's body was any more tense, she'd be pluperfect.

Charlotte ceased moving until Stephanie's hand slid off her arm, and then proceeded to uncork the bottle.

"Sit down," said Declan, motioning toward the sofa.

Charlotte uncorked the bottle before he could return to the kitchen island.

"I'm so sorry," he whispered.

The angry wrinkles carved in Charlotte's forehead smoothed and it looked as though she might burst into giggles. He relaxed, knowing they'd laugh about Stephanie's visit later. She poured three glasses and he delivered one to Stephanie.

"Thank you," she said, taking it.

"Now tell us what's wrong," he said, sitting at the other end of the L-shaped sofa, a spot as far away from Stephanie as he could find.

Stephanie stared at Charlotte, who sat beside him. "I guess I could use *your* help as well," she said, taking a sip.

"*Fantastic*, can't wait," said Charlotte, taking a long sip of her own.

Stephanie seemed to brace herself and then began her tale. "Remember I told you I had a client who had information about the recent killings?"

"Yes."

"She's trying to kill me."

"The killer?" asked Declan.

"My *client*."

"You? Why?"

"The person who put the alligator in that man's pool, and stabbed the crossword guy in the neck—he's doing those things to get the attention of my client."

"And the poisonings?" asked Charlotte.

Stephanie's eyes grew a little wider. "Um, not that one."

Charlotte scowled. "Why would he kill people to attract your client?"

"She's the Puzzle Killer."

Charlotte gasped and put down her wine glass so quickly it sloshed on to the table. "So the *Puzzle Killer* did the poisoning?"

Stephanie shook her head. "I'm not at liberty to share information like that about my client."

"But you just told us she's the Puzzle Killer—"

"I found out she was the Puzzle Killer before she hired me, so technically that's not covered."

"Oh. But she told you she poisoned those people after she hired you."

"Right. I mean..." Stephanie sniffed. "If she had, it would have happened after she hired me. *Hypothetically*."

"I'll take that for a *yes*." Charlotte pumped her fist and whispered, '*Frank was right!*'

Declan smirked as he watched Charlotte dork out and then turned to Stephanie. "You said *she*. The Puzzle Killer is a woman?"

"Yes. And this other killer is blackmailing her to commit a new murder. He's gathered evidence against her."

"And he chose *you* as the victim?" asked Charlotte.

Stephanie nodded her head toward the suitcase. "Now you can see why I can't go home." Her gaze drifted to Declan and she lowered her eyelids.

Bedroom eyes.

He felt a wave of panic.

"I wonder why he chose you," mumbled Charlotte, seemingly oblivious to the exchange. Declan dropped his hand on his girlfriend's thigh and stared pointedly back at Stephanie.

"Maybe he's one of your ex-boyfriends?" he

suggested. "That would explain his blood lust."

"Very funny," said Stephanie, standing and walking to the wine on the counter. "But to be honest, it's not much of a mystery why Alex chose me."

"Because you're the Puzzle Killer's lawyer?" asked Charlotte.

Stephanie refilled her glass and returned. "Because I'm her *daughter.*"

Charlotte and Declan's jaws both fell.

"You're the Puzzle Killer's *daughter?*" echoed Charlotte.

"Suddenly so much makes sense," mumbled Declan. "*No*...wait...your mother just died and there's no *way* Miss Debbie was the Puzzle Killer. I mean, she was crazy, but—"

"Debbie *adopted* me. My *real* mother is alive and trying to kill me."

"What's her name?" asked Charlotte.

Stephanie twisted her lips to the right. "I can't say."

"Can't or won't."

"Both."

"But you're sure she intends to kill you?"

"I just met her for the first time a couple of weeks ago and I thought we were reconnecting pretty well, but between the electric chair and *me*, well, I dunno. She *is* a serial killer, after all."

Charlotte sighed. "But killing your own daughter? How do you know? Maybe she has no intention of killing you. She obviously told you who she is; she must trust you."

"And she *told* you about Alex," added Declan. "Why would she *tell* you she's going to have to kill you for him?"

Stephanie shot back the last of her second glass of wine. "She didn't tell me."

"Then how do you know all this?"

"Let's just say I have my sources, and my sources say she's not planning on going to jail anytime soon. The fact that she told me who she *is*, is just another reason for her to want me dead."

Declan's gaze moved to Stephanie's suitcase. "So you were planning to stay *here*?"

"If that's okay," said Stephanie, her voice soft.

Declan looked at Charlotte, who stood.

"You'll stay with me."

Stephanie's head swiveled. "Huh?"

"Your mother found you, so she knows about you. She might know that you and Declan dated."

Declan made an "ack" noise at the memory of his time with Stephanie and she glared at him.

"The point is," continued Charlotte. "It isn't safe for you to be here. Not for either of you; so you can stay with me. If she knows about Declan, *my* house is the last place on Earth she'd look for you."

Stephanie remained speechless, her lip curled, staring at Charlotte as if she were asking her to help unclog a toilet.

"I, I have to use the ladies," she said, striding across the room and disappearing down the hall.

"So what are the chances this is all a ruse to

plant herself in your house?" asked Charlotte once they heard the bathroom door shut.

"Fifty-fifty. I'm glad you're here for *so* many reasons. I don't think I could have kicked her to the curb on the off chance this is real, but you devised the perfect solution."

Charlotte chuckled. "Maybe for *you*. I just asked a succubus to be my roommate."

Declan hugged her. "You're the best."

"I am."

He kissed her and then leaned away as a thought popped into his head. "Oh, hey! While I have a moment with you, did I tell you about Lester?'

"Lester? The guy who's been hitting on Auntie Carolina?"

"You know about that?"

She nodded. "He's got it bad. Mariska says it's because of Carolina's massive boobs."

"Okay, I didn't need to hear that."

"Sorry."

"Anyway, Lester is on our bowling team and he freaked out last night. Said his car was broken and asked for a ride home. Next thing I know, the cops pull me over and take him away."

"Why?"

"I don't know, but they were clearly there for him in the first place. Lester got into my back seat and *laid down*."

"Oh my. I guess Auntie Carolina's instincts are right on. She doesn't want any part of him."

They heard a flush and Stephanie re-entered. Her

expression twisted and she sniffed.

"Do you smell smoke?" she asked.

Declan's attention shot to the stove. Around the edge of the oven door dark smoke slithered like snakes.

"My chicken!" he yelped, running to the stove.

"Time to switch to red wine," said Stephanie. "Looks like we're having pizza."

CHAPTER TWENTY-TWO

Charlotte returned home and found her door unlocked. Inside, she found Mariska and Carolina sitting in her kitchen, chatting over coffee. Abby trotted up to her, tail wagging, and gave her kneecaps a sniff. She spotted the naked cat flopped over Carolina's shoulder.

"Looks like you have a friend," she said. "I guess I'm going to have to name that thing."

"Mister Coppertone," said Carolina, reaching up to scratch the cat's face. Charlotte could hear it purring from ten feet away.

"What?"

"Remember the Coppertone ads with the dog pulling the little girl's bikini bottoms down to show her tan line?"

"I've seen them in old movies. I don't so much *remember* them."

"I named him Mister Coppertone because he has a naked butt."

"Isn't that great?" asked Mariska. "Plus, who would need sunblock more than a furless cat?"

Charlotte raised one eyebrow. "Why *Mister* Coppertone?"

Carolina looked at her like she was crazy.

"Because he's a boy cat."

"Right. Of course. So, what are you two doing here?"

"We're hiding from the Bourbon Club," said Mariska.

"Men drinking are about as stupid as things can get," muttered Carolina.

Stephanie entered behind Charlotte.

"Who is *she*?" asked Carolina, eyeballing Stephanie as if she smelled funny.

"She's..." Charlotte thought about her answer. There was no way to explain that she was harboring her boyfriend's ex-girlfriend because her mother was trying to kill her—without Carolina's head exploding. She looked at Mariska, and found her staring at her, shaking her head ever so slightly, as if begging her not to offer any explanation that would set off her sister.

"She's a friend of mine," said Charlotte.

Stephanie's gaze swept the room and as it passed the pink cat leering from Carolina's shoulder, she flinched. "For the love of—what is *that*?"

"Mister Coppertone. Long story." Charlotte turned her attention to the ladies. "Stephanie is going to stay here while her apartment is being painted."

"She's—" Mariska sounded alarmed but cut herself short by slapping her hand over her mouth.

Subtle. She obviously remembered Stephanie.

"Hi," Mariska added, removing her hand to offer a tiny wave in Stephanie's direction.

"Hi," said Stephanie.

"You *hired* someone to paint your apartment?" asked Carolina. "Painting is easy. You could have saved a lot of money. What are you paying them?"

Stephanie looked at Charlotte and she returned the stare with a hard look she hoped telegraphed *play along*.

Stephanie sighed. "They're friends of mine. They're doing it for a case of beer."

"Beer," muttered Carolina. "I hope you didn't buy it for them *before* they finished or it will never get done."

"What colors did you decid on?" asked Mariska.

Charlotte squinted at her and Mariska bit her lip, looking as though she'd realized she'd been sucked into a lie that didn't need extra details, like paint color. "Nevermind. It doesn't matter," she mumbled.

Carolina was still staring at Stephanie.

Stephanie stared back.

Carolina squinted.

Oh no.

"What kind of skirt is that?" asked Carolina, pointing at Stephanie's above-the-knee outfit.

"It's a Valli," said Stephanie.

"Frankie?"

"*Giambattista.*"

Carolina snorted. "What's that? Mexican?"

"Italian."

"Where'd you get it?"

"Why?"

"You should go back and get the rest of it." Carolina started cackling and though Mariska tried to restrain her laughter, a moment later she began tittering as well.

Stephanie took a step forward. "It's a nine hundred dollar—"

"*Don't*," said Charlotte, touching Stephanie's arm. "Let's take your things to the guest room."

Stephanie huffed and snatched her overnight bag from the ground. With one last glare at Carolina she turned to follow Charlotte down the hall, but she didn't make it far. Instead, she bumped into Charlotte, both of them nearly falling.

"Smooth," called Carolina. Mariska giggled.

"What are you doing?" hissed Stephanie.

Charlotte plucked something from the floor and held it up. It was an earring, with a blue stone in the center, encircled by tiny pearls.

"Did you lose an earring?"

Stephanie felt her ear lobe with the hand not holding her bag.

"I did." She covered her ear with her hair and held out her palm.

Charlotte reached up and pushed back Stephanie's hair, revealing a silver shell earring. The other ear was already visible and sporting the shell's twin. "You're *wearing* two earrings."

"Uh huh."

"Neither of which look like this one."

"It must have come out of my bag."

"*Out of your bag?*"

"Or it was on my bag. I packed in a hurry. I probably knocked one *on* to my bag. It's definitely mine though. One of my favorites. Thank you for finding it."

Charlotte pursed her lips. Stephanie was lying, this she knew. But the earring wasn't hers. She walked past Stephanie and showed the jewelry to Mariska and Carolina.

"Did one of you lose an earring?"

They peered at it and both shook their heads.

"That's beautiful," said Mariska. "I *wish* it was mine."

Charlotte sighed and returned to Stephanie who again thrust out her palm. She placed the earring into it and walked past her to the guest room.

Stephanie followed. "Your friends are charming," she said, her voice dripping with sarcasm.

Abby entered and, having not received her obligatory pets from the visitor, pushed her head into Stephanie's knees. She extended her leg to push away the dog.

"Carolina is what we like to call *opinionated*," said Charlotte.

"She's what I like to call a b—"

"Hey," said Charlotte, holding up her hand. "She's basically my aunt, so watch it."

"Fine."

"And if you push my dog again I'm going to tie you to the post office flag pole with a sign around your neck that says *Come and get me*."

"I might prefer that," grumbled Stephanie staring at the bed. "What's the count on these sheets?"

"Two. The flat one and the one that's impossible

to fold."

There was a knock at the front door and Abby, who had been skulking nearby waiting for a second chance at Stephanie, ripped out of the room, barking.

"It's like grand central station in this place," said Stephanie. "How can anyone live like this?"

Charlotte ignored her and went to answer the door. She found Carolina had beaten her to it, the cat still perched on her shoulder like a pirate's parrot.

"Who are you?" said Carolina, her tone implying the visitor better have an *excellent* answer.

"I'm—"

"That's Seamus," said Charlotte peering over Carolina's shoulder. "He's Declan's uncle and my quasi-boss." She shooed Carolina out of the way. The cat growled at her.

"Oh, your boss stops by at night?" asked Carolina, her eyebrows so high on her forehead they forgot what her eyes looked like. She stood her ground at the entrance, eyeing Seamus up and down.

"You could be her father," she hissed at him.

Seamus winked. "Nah, she's too good lookin' to be my daughter."

Carolina grunted and returned to Mariska's side, her lips pressed in a tight, white line as her sister attempted to explain Seamus' innocent relationship with Charlotte.

"You shouldn't taunt her," whispered Charlotte to Seamus. "We don't poke the bull."

"She knows she has a baboon's ass on her shoulder, right?" Seamus grinned at his own joke, but his smile melted like butter in a hot pan. His gaze had drifted past Charlotte, and she turned to find Stephanie standing there.

"What's *she* doin' here?" he asked, taking a step inside.

Charlotte shot Carolina a glance and pushed Seamus back. She followed him outside and shut the door behind her.

"Are you runnin' a home for abandoned harpies now?" he asked.

As quickly and quietly as she could, Charlotte explained Stephanie's homicidal matriarch.

"So...the person doin' all the killing was trying to get the attention of the Puzzle Killer, who happens to be Stephanie's real mother?" Seamus said, his voice growing higher in pitch with every word.

"In a nutshell."

"Does she know anything else about this person pullin' her mother's strings?"

"She said his name is Alex. Oh, and Stephanie's mom is probably responsible for the poisonings."

"She said that?"

"It was implied that those deaths were her mother's answer to Alex."

Seamus rubbed his hand across his hair. "Alex. Well, I guess that's somethin' to tell Simone. I don't think she'll pay us for it, but it's a lead. Maybe she knows one of her WitSec people is obsessed with the Puzzle Killer. This could be something."

"Maybe. That would be good. If we could lock up whoever is blackmailing Stephanie's mother, then she won't have any reason to kill Stephanie."

"Well, now that you mention it, we don't have to rush or anything—"

Charlotte shook her head. "That's not funny."

"Sorry. I'm kidding." He shook his head.

"What is it?"

"I dunno. I'm thinking when you find out your mother is trying to kill you, your first thought isn't how to *stop* her. It's *how could my own mother be trying to kill me.*"

"Yeah, that's an ouchy for sure."

"How's she doin'?"

She shrugged. "She's as warm and fuzzy as ever. Unfased. When I got to Declan's she was crying, but I think that was more for his benefit than any true outpouring of emotion. Plan A was for her to stay with *him* and I'm afraid I interfered."

"Aye, I've seen her waterworks before. Declan's soft-hearted, but I'd like to think isn't an idiot. Still, probably best you were there. We're all mostly idiots."

Charlotte smiled. "What're you here for, anyway?"

"Oh, I was over at Jackie's and thought I'd walk by and ask you if you wanted to come with me to that puzzle maker's house tomorrow to see if we can find anything. But this new information changes all that. I'm going to swing by and tell Simone what we know first."

"Everything good with Jackie?"

Seamus scowled. "Yes, why?"

She shrugged. "Just making conversation."

"Hm."

There was a yell from inside.

"I guess I better get back in there," said Charlotte, opening the door.

Seamus saluted her and headed down the driveway.

Charlotte found Mariska clapping. Stephanie and Carolina were both rubbing their arms. Carolina's massive smile threatened to split her face in two.

"What is going on?" asked Charlotte.

"Carolina beat Stephanie arm wrestling," said Mariska.

"*Arm wrestling?*"

"I never turn down a challenge," said Stephanie. "But then, I've never been about brute strength. I'm more about *finesse*."

"I'm more about *winning*," said Carolina. She high-fived Mariska. As she leaned forward Mister Coppertone took a swipe at Stephanie, who backed away just in time.

Charlotte couldn't believe the cat who had been such a wimp since arriving, suddenly seemed like a little tough guy.

"I'll kill you next time," said Stephanie. She grinned at Carolina and headed down the hall.

Carolina watched as she left and then looked at Charlotte. "Keep an eye on that one."

"Oh, I know," said Charlotte, rolling her eyes.

"*We know,*" echoed Mariska, mimicking Charlotte's eye roll. "You know what? She once tried to steal a costume contest from us—"

Carolina shook her head and cut her sister short. "There's something *off* about her."

"Yeah the rest of her skirt!" said Mariska, slapping her sister's shoulder. The two of them started laughing and Charlotte closed her eyes. It was going to be a long night.

CHAPTER TWENTY-THREE

Seamus knocked on Simone's door, making a mental note to stay on his toes. The last time he'd visited her house he'd ended up handcuffed to her wall. There would be no funny business this time. He was here on *official* business.

Simone opened the door and stared at him through the screen. "Yes?"

"I've got some information for you."

Simone opened the outer door and stepped on to the porch. Without speaking, she brushed past him and he jumped.

"Are you well?" she asked.

"Fine. Fine," muttered Seamus.

She sat on a built-in bench and crossed her legs. "Tell me your news."

"I've got some information about those killings."

"You know who's doing them?"

"No. But I can tell you *why* he's doing them. I thought if you knew *that*, you could see if it rang any bells for you and your witness protection people."

She nodded. "Sounds good. Go on."

Seamus eyed the bench on which Simone sat. It was small, and the only seating available. He rocked forward with every intention of sitting beside her, and then rocked back, unsure that was the right move. This happened several more times.

"Why does it look like you're on a ship?" asked Simone.

"Sorry. I, er..." He took a step back and leaned against the railing. "This is good."

"I'm so happy. Tell me your news."

"Right. My nephew's ex-girlfriend came by his house yesterday. She said her *mother* is trying to kill her because the person who killed the puzzle fella and the alligator fella is forcing her to do it."

Simone scowled. "What? I don't understand you."

"Sorry, that was confusing. My nephew's ex-girlfriend's name is Stephanie. She's a bit of a nutter, so we aren't always inclined to believe her. But she seems genuinely worried for her safety."

"Did you say her *mother* is trying to kill her?"

Seamus nodded. "That's not even the craziest part."

"Oh, I can't wait to hear what *that* is."

"Her mother is the Puzzle Killer."

Simone gasped. "You're kidding!"

"That's what she says. She says the guy who did the other killings only did them to get the attention of the Puzzle Killer. When he finally contacted her, he told her she had to *kill her own daughter* or he'd turn her into the police."

"That's *horrible*."

"Aye."

"And you believe this Stephanie?"

"I think so. This seems too crazy for her to make up."

"Why doesn't she turn her in?"

"I don't think she has any actual proof. Plus, she's a lawyer. The woman is her client now."

"How does she know all this? Did her mother threaten her?"

"She didn't say how she knew—said she had *sources*—but now she's hiding from her own mother."

Simone tossed her head, eyes rolling. "This is insane!"

"Yup."

"Is she safe for now? Is she with your nephew?"

"No, they thought this killer fella might know Declan was her ex, so she's staying with Dec's new girlfriend."

Simone chuckled. "That sounds uncomfortable."

"You have no idea. So, does this ring any bells for you? Have I given you something you can use?"

She shook her head. "No. None of my WitSec people have ever mentioned any interest in the Puzzle Killer. My people tend to kill for profit, not fun."

"I guess that's good."

"Not really. If I saw a connection I'd have a path to explore."

"True."

"Is there any chance this person will make the connection between your nephew and his *new* girlfriend?"

"I guess it's possible." Seamus pondered this. "I

didn't think so, but now that you mention it this guy seems to know a lot of things he shouldn't."

"That's what I'm thinking. Maybe you should bring her *here*."

"Stephanie? You'd take her in?"

Simone shrugged. "Yes, if it would help. Though none of this sounds like it's the handiwork of one of my charges, I still feel a tiny bit responsible for anything criminal that happens in Charity."

"I'll let Charlotte know."

"Charlotte?"

"My nephew's current girlfriend."

"Ah." Simone stood and strolled toward Seamus. She placed a palm on his chest and he froze, like a mongoose held in the gaze of a cobra.

She leaned in and kissed him.

He didn't stop her.

She pulled back slowly, his lower lip held gently in her teeth. She released and his lip snapped back into place.

"Good luck with everything. Let me know if you need me," she purred.

He pursed his lips and nodded stiffly.

Simone went back inside and Seamus looked up in time to spot a face staring at him from a parked car.

A very familiar parked car.

Charlotte's parked car.

He hung his head.

"Bugger."

CHAPTER TWENTY-FOUR

Charlotte had left to run an errand and Stephanie found herself alone in Bland-ville, hoping the *Golden Girls* didn't swing by for tea.

She rubbed her face. *This is a nightmare.* The whole point of hiding was to *stay with Declan* where he'd be unable to resist her charms for long. Instead, she was living with his *girlfriend*, her dog, the most revolting cat she'd ever seen and a revolving cast of geriatrics.

She wandered into the living room and pulled her phone from her pocket before sitting. She stared at it for a few minutes and then dialed.

"Hello?"

"Hi."

There was a pause before Jamie's voice perked a notch. "Hey! Hi, dear. I was just going to call you—"

Stephanie swallowed. "Call? Or *kill?*"

"I'm sorry, what?"

"Is today the day you're going to kill me? I just need to know for my calendar."

There was another silence before Jamie answered in a much more serious tone. "You monitored my interaction with Alex?"

"I did."

"How?"

"*How*? You think I can give you a super secure computer for your homicidal maniac Match.com and I can't trace what happens?"

"I am never going to understand computers," said Jamie, sounding exhausted. "It all sounds like magic to me."

"Not nearly as magical as watching your mother agree to kill you."

Jamie scoffed. "Oh *stop*. I don't have any intention of killing you. I'm just delaying him while I figure out my next move."

"Can I ask you why you were in Declan's girlfriend's house?"

"What?"

"She found an earring. A sapphire surrounded by pearls. Sound familiar?"

"Oh! You found my earring! *Hallelujah*. I spent three hours searching for that thing. That is a *load* off my mind. It must have been that stupid cat—"

"Why were you in Charlotte's house?"

"You know, basic surveillance. Wanted to get a handle on her, just in case—"

"In case *what*?"

"Well, for one, what if I killed *you* in a fire for Alex, but the body was actually Charlotte's? Huh? Ever think of that?"

"Mom, it isn't nineteen seventy. They'll be able to tell the body isn't mine in about two seconds. Seriously, don't you ever watch *Dateline*?"

"I've actually been on *Dateline*. Sort of. Look,

why don't you swing by and we'll talk? We'll figure out something—"

"Said the spider to the fly. No thanks. I'm staying as far away from you as I can."

"Come on, honey! We just got reconnected. You can't—"

Stephanie hung up and let her gaze drift around Charlotte's sad little living room. It looked like Declan's pawnshop threw up in it.

She heard a low, soft growl and noticed the cat had left its usual perch on the refrigerator and made its way to the chair beside her. It stared at her and she could see muscles flexing beneath its naked skin, as if it were planning to jump.

She scowled at it.

"Don't even think about it."

The cat hissed and slinked from the chair before scurrying back to the refrigerator.

Someone knocked on the front door and Stephanie stood. Abby flew down the hallway, barking. Stephanie spotted an old man with large teeth peering at her through the window. *Great. Another old person.* It was like Charlotte handed out free heart medication or something.

Using her leg to push back the dog, she opened the door.

"Yes?"

"Hi. It's me, Lester. I need to talk to you."

Stephanie raised an eyebrow. "You do?"

"It's about my arrest. I need you to get a message

to Carolina."

"Your arrest? This is getting interesting."

"I need you to let her know it wasn't anything important. I mean, it turned out to be, in a way, but not really. Can you tell her it wasn't anything important?"

Stephanie smiled. *The old dude thinks I'm Charlotte.* This could be a chance to have some fun.

"Well, this all depends, Lester. Why *were* you arrested?"

He sighed and hung his head. "An alligator."

"An alligator?"

"It ate someone."

Stephanie straightened. "Who?"

"Some guy. In a pool."

"The guy in the paper? The puzzle maker?"

He nodded.

"What do *you* have to do with it?"

"I was supposed to be watching the alligator. His name was Oscar. I took a part-time job at Gary's Gator House and I guess I left the cage open."

His eyes shifted and Stephanie's sixth sense told her he was lying. "The Gator House is thirty miles from here, isn't it? You're telling me that alligator walked thirty miles to slide into some guy's pool? On those stubby little legs?"

"Gators can run twenty miles per hour," said Lester.

"I'll remember that next time I'm near one of your cages."

Lester scratched his cheek. "It sounds crazy, I

don't understand it either, but Oscar was tagged so they know it was him. He's one of the oldest at the park. Or, he *was*. They killed him after the...the *mishap*."

"And you left his cage door open?"

"I guess. Well, sort of." He shuffled and thrust his hands in his pockets. "Can I be honest?"

"By all means."

"I told the cops when I got home after work I found the padlock in my pocket. By the time I drove back, Oscar was missing."

"But that's not what happened?"

"No. Some guy paid me a thousand bucks to turn my back on the cage for a few minutes."

"And *he* stole the alligator?"

Lester shrugged. "I guess. I left and never went back. That's why they came looking for me at the bowling alley. They thought I stole Oscar."

"Arrested at the bowling alley," mumbled Stephanie. "Oh, the glamor of it all."

"Not exactly the bowling alley," said Lester, staring off into the distance. "They spotted me in Declan's car."

Stephanie's eyes grew wide. "Declan? How is he involved in this?"

"He's on our bowling team."

Stephanie blanched. "Ew. She's really got him domesticated now, doesn't she?"

"Who?"

"Charlotte."

"Charlotte? But you're..." He leaned forward and

peered into her face. "Wait, didn't you used to have dark hair?"

"Not since I was seventeen."

"You're *not* Charlotte?"

"No. And frankly I'm horrified you thought I was."

"Oh, oh jeeze. Look, don't tell Carolina anything, okay?"

Stephanie crossed her arms over her chest. "Lester, let me ask you something."

"Sure."

"Did you know the guy who stole the alligator? Could you describe him?"

"Sure, he was a big guy, lots of tats. He had one with a mermaid, but it had the face of an angel, with a halo, you know? I thought that was different."

"But you didn't tell the cops that?"

"No. Not yet anyway. I'm hoping this is the end of it, but worst case scenario I can give up the guy and make a deal."

Stephanie nodded. "Smart. I'm a criminal defense lawyer, you know."

Lester's eyes grew wide. "You are?"

"Yep. I'm sort of on, *vacation*, but why don't we swing to my office and I can give you some counseling that could save you a lot of jail time?"

Lester slapped his hands together. "Oh, that would be wonderful! But... Can't we just do it here?"

"I don't want to run the risk of Charlotte or—worse—Carolina showing up, do you?"

"No. No, that wouldn't be good." Lester

grinned. "Let's go!

CHAPTER TWENTY-FIVE

"Hello there," said Seamus, strolling to Charlotte's car. "What brings you to Silver Lake? Aren't you permanently banned from there after staging the great dog poop revolt?"

"Very funny. How's your lip?"

"Ah, you saw that, did you?"

Charlotte nodded.

"It isn't what it looks like. She's mental." Seamus pointed his finger to his head and made circles to emphasize his point.

"Let's not drag this out. Are you cheating on Jackie?"

"Cheating? First of all, we never said we were exclusive—"

"Wait, let me stop you right there," said Charlotte holding up her hand. "You mean you and Jackie *didn't* have a document signed by a notary stating that you're exclusively dating each other?"

Seamus grinned. "See? You understand."

"No—I'm kidding—but there *are* certain assumptions people make. For one, I'm thinking Jackie assumes that you're not kissing ladies on their porches."

"I didn't kiss a lady on a porch. A lady kissed

me."

Charlotte stared at him.

"Seriously. I can't tell you it isn't beguiling that Simone gets a little handsy with me, but I'm not an *idiot*. I'm too old for that kind of trouble. And I'm *not* cheating on Jackie."

Charlotte smiled. "Good."

"So let me ask you this, Miss Uncomplicated, why are you here?"

Charlotte knit her brow. "Well, now, that *is* complicated..."

Seamus pointed at her. "You're *spying* on me!"

"Maybe. A little."

"Jackie thinks I'm cheating, doesn't she? Did she ask you to tail me?"

"No! Absolutely not. She just happened to share certain *questions* she had with me and I took it upon myself."

"Sounds pretty cloak and dagger to me. Pretty *complicated*."

Charlotte chuckled. "Now that this is all behind us, what did Simone say?"

"Nice segue. Smooth."

"Thank you."

"Simone doesn't think any of her people are the sort to try and trap the Puzzle Killer."

"Hm. That's too bad. Would have made life easier."

"Yes, it would have. But as long as I have you here, she also said she'd be willing to watch Stephanie for us."

Charlotte perked. "Really?"

"She thinks your house isn't the safest place. It's feasible Stephanie's mother could follow the strings to you."

"That thought crossed my mind last night when I found Mariska and her sister at my house. It's one thing to put myself in danger; it's another to endanger everyone else."

"So we're agreed? We'll bring Stephanie to Simone?"

She nodded. "Probably a good idea. There's no way to trace Stephanie to Simone unless someone's following me."

They both looked down the street behind Charlotte's car.

"I should probably get out of here."

He nodded.

Charlotte drove home to find no one there. She was tempted to laze around the house and enjoy the emptiness of it but there was too much to do. She had to find Stephanie, who should have been there. And once that was accomplished, she had to let Jackie know her fears were unfounded. At least when it came to Simone.

She walked outside and stood on the porch. *Did Stephanie take a walk?* She wasn't sure where to look first. She pulled out her phone and on her recent call list, saw Declan's name.

Ah. That would be a good place to start.

She was about to dial when a blur of brown

whizzed over her sandaled toes and she yelped as what felt suspiciously like a dog's toenail dug into the top of her foot.

"Turbo!"

Darla headed towards her, dressed in a flowing mumu and moving about as fast as Charlotte had ever seen her.

"Grab that hot dog!" she screamed.

Charlotte followed the blur and saw Darla's new miniature dachshund looping around for another pass. When he neared, she squatted and scooped the squirming pipsqueak into her arms.

"Cheese and crackers," said Darla. "That dog is going to be the death of me."

Charlotte handed the panting bundle of energy over to Darla, who snuggled the puppy against her cheek.

"You look furious," said Charlotte, smirking.

"Oh, he's just so dang cute. What are you up to today?"

"I'm looking for Stephanie."

"Is that the blonde?"

Charlotte nodded.

Darla shook her head and made a disapproving *tsk* noise. "Mariska told me all about it. That girl is up to no good. Carolina called her a Jezebel."

"Carolina calls everyone a Jezebel, though I'm inclined to agree this time. Still, right now, I need to find Jezzy. She's supposed to be *here*."

"She left with Lester."

Charlotte scowled. "What?"

"Lester. The new guy. I saw them out here on the porch talking and then they toddled off together."

"On foot?"

She nodded.

Charlotte put her fingers over her lips as a thought occurred to her. "Oh no."

"What is it?"

"Did you know Lester was arrested the other night?"

Darla's eyes grew wide. "No! Why?"

"I don't know." Charlotte hopped into her ruby red golf cart. "Where is he again? The old section?"

"I think so. I'm not sure what house though."

"Okay. Gotta go."

Charlotte pulled out of the driveway and mashed the pedal to the floor. Rounding the first turn, she spotted Jackie watering what was left of her garden in the distance.

"He's not cheating!" she screamed as she approached.

Jackie turned to watch her whiz past. "No?"

"No!"

"Good!"

Charlotte smiled. *Check that off the to-do list.* She loved multitasking.

She racked her brain for everything she'd heard about Lester. She knew he was living in the old section but where...where...*Tilladay's house.* That's right. He was renting Mr. Tilladay's house.

She cocked her head. *Where did Mr. Tilladay go*

anyway? Had she heard?

Oh, I hope he isn't walled up in the house or something.

She pulled onto Alpinia Lane in the older section of Pineapple Port and into the driveway of Mr. Tilladay's former house. There was no car in the carport. She hopped out and knocked on the door.

Nothing.

She peered through the window, but saw no movement. No one seemed to be there.

Pulling out her phone she called Declan.

"Have you seen Stephanie?" she asked when he answered.

"No, isn't she at your house?"

"No. Darla said she saw her go somewhere with Lester."

"Lester from bowling?"

"Yep."

"Why would she go anywhere with Lester?"

"I have no idea. I'm at his house now but there's no one here."

Declan fell silent as they both thought on any possible relationship between Lester and Stephanie.

"Maybe he needed a lawyer," said Charlotte.

"For his police trouble? That's not a bad thought. Did you check her office?"

"No. I'll go borrow Mariska's car and check it out."

"Okay. Let me know if you need any help. Be careful."

"I will."

Charlotte hung up and hopped back in her golf

cart.

"One of these days I'm going to have to buy a car, like a big girl," she mumbled, stomping on the pedal.

CHAPTER TWENTY-SIX

Stephanie and Lester took his car to her one-story, cement brick office building. The building was unmarked, and she stared at the spot her sign should be. She hadn't decided what to call the firm yet.

Ah well. Now wasn't the time to design a logo.

She motioned him to a parking spot in front of the door.

"Do you mind backing in? It's a quirk of mine."

Lester shrugged and made a K-turn so he could back his car up to the door.

Before he could turn off the car and get out, she hopped out and jogged around the side of the office. She found a wheelbarrow there and pushed it to the door. Leaving it beside the entrance, she wiggled her key in the lock before pointing Lester inside. He obliged, and she pushed the wheelbarrow in behind him, parking it in the sparse reception area. She hadn't hired a receptionist yet. For now it was easier and cheaper to answer the phone with a deep southern accent and then pretend to patch through to herself.

"Why are you putting that in here?" Lester asked, staring at the wheelbarrow.

"Just in case."

"You think it might be stolen outside?"

She shrugged. "Sure. Come into my office."

She clapped the dirt from her hands and led Lester into her office.

"Nice," he said, looking around his plush surroundings.

"Thanks," she took a moment to admire her own decorating. She'd bought everything from the unique riveted chairs to the classic leather sofa at Restoration Hardware, which was one of the reasons she'd yet to hire a receptionist. One more trip there and she'd be eating Ramen noodles for the rest of the year.

"Have a seat."

Stephanie moved to the window and peeked through the shutter slats. She didn't want to stay long enough for her mother to cruise by. She sighed and closed the blinds. *Maybe being here is a bad idea.* She surveyed every drawer and knick-knack as a potential weapon. When the Puzzle Killer was after you, anything could be a trap.

She shook her head. *No. It was too soon.* Her mother hadn't had time to plan an interesting killing. At this point her greatest worries were knives, guns and poisons. The classics.

Stepping between Lester and his view of the bookshelf, she slid a legal encyclopedia from the shelf and pressed against the side wall with her fingertips. A hidden door popped open and from it, she pulled a small vial with a black top. She closed the trapdoor and slid the book back into place.

Turning, she found Lester staring at the bottle of bourbon on her credenza.

"Fancy a glass?" she asked.

Lester grinned. "Are you saying it's five o'clock somewhere?"

"If I am, *kill* me," she mumbled.

She hoisted a crystal tumbler, surreptitiously wiped the worst of the dust out of it, and poured half a glass.

"Ice?" he asked.

"Excuse me?"

"Do you have any ice?"

She pointed. "See the freezer over there?"

Lester twisted in his chair and scanned the back wall of the office. "Um, no?"

"Then no. I don't have any ice."

He smiled and held out his hand. "Then neat is just fine."

She picked up a shot glass labeled "Joe's Pub" and poured another. Picking up the crystal tumbler, she took a step toward Lester and paused, holding the glass just out of his reach.

"How much do you weigh, Lester?"

"Is that important to the case?"

"It could be. I like to cover my bases."

"About a hundred and forty-five pounds."

She nodded and handed him the glass. "Okay. Good."

They clinked and she shot back hers.

He took a large sip. "Wonderful, is this Jim Beam?"

She dropped her head and looked at him from beneath her brow. "Pappy Van Winkle, but close."

"Hm." He took another sip. "So, what should we do about my predicament?"

She leaned against the desk. "Well, for one I think you should stick with your story about accidentally leaving the cage open. It would be difficult to prove you didn't."

"So you don't think I should tell them about the guy who paid me?"

"No. Definitely not."

"But what if they catch the guy and he turns on *me*?"

"They won't."

"How do you know?"

"Trust me."

"I—" Lester gripped the armrest. "Wow. I'm not feeling well at all."

"No? Maybe we should get you home. Stand up." Stephanie moved to his side and began tugging on his arm.

Lester stood. "I don't know. I...I think I might be sick."

"Then we *definitely* need to get you off this rug."

She dragged him out into the hall.

"I'm really dizzy." His eyes began to flutter and he started to tilt as if he was going to fall.

Stephanie pushed him so he landed neatly in the wheelbarrow.

He gasped when he hit the metal and slapped one hand on his heart.

"Elevated heart rate?" she asked.

His mouth moved, but no sound escaped. A moment later, he was unconscious.

There was a knock on the door and Stephanie jumped. She circled the wheelbarrow and pushed it toward the spare office. Lester's arm, flopping over the side, knocked into a vase of flowers on the table near the sofa and it crashed to the floor.

Stephanie grit her teeth and cursed. She got half into the office when his arm caught against the wall and nearly tipped the wheelbarrow.

There was another knock on the door, this one louder.

"Coming!" she screamed. She backed up and pushed Lester's flopping arm across his chest and tried again.

She hit something and the wheelbarrow stopped so suddenly she almost fell into it. She peeked over the edge and saw she'd wheeled right into the pale, dead arm of the corpse occupying her spare office. The one with the angel mermaid tattoo.

"Lester, I believe you've met Jake," she mumbled, tipping the wheelbarrow over and dropping Lester on top of the now deceased man she'd hired to steal the alligator.

The other loose end.

She twisted the barrow out of the way and closed the door.

Whew. It was time to take out the trash. Jake was getting ripe.

She pushed the larger pieces of the vase under

the sofa with her foot and ran to the door.

Before opening it, she peeked through the front shutters, and spotted a dark-haired woman.

Charlotte.

Stephanie threw back her head, screwed shut her eyes and pounded an invisible table with both fists. *Why is this girl always ruining everything?*

She took a moment to compose herself and opened the door.

"Well hello, Charlotte, fancy meeting you here."

Charlotte put her hands on her hips. "Stephanie, what are you doing here? You're supposed to be at *my* house. Don't you think this will be the first place your mother looks for you?"

Stephanie nodded. "You're right, you're right—I just needed to pick up a few things."

"Is Lester here?"

"Who?"

"Lester. Guy from Pineapple Port. Darla said you left with him."

"Oh! Lester. Old guy. No. He wanted to show me a sandhill crane. Like I've never seen one of those before." She laughed and threw her hand in the air to show Charlotte how little her interaction with Lester had meant to her.

Charlotte stood on her toes and peered into the office. "Your office looks nice."

"This is my future reception. You should see my—" Stephanie tried to stop herself but knew it was too late. Charlotte breezed by her into the office.

"I'd love to see it," she said, her eyes drifting to

the shards of broken vase on the ground near the sofa. "Whoops."

"Furniture delivery guys knocked it over," said Stephanie. She held the doorknob and chewed her lip. She wanted to keep the door *open* in order to better usher Charlotte out of the office, but on the other hand, if her mother was on the way to *kill* her, she didn't want to make it *too* easy for her.

At least sweet Charlotte would probably end up collateral damage in that scenario. She could die happy knowing that.

Still.

"I'll give you the nickel tour," she said, closing and locking the front door.

"Great," said Charlotte, walking towards the spare office.

"No!" Stephanie lunged toward her and Charlotte froze. "That's, that's not the right office. It's this one. That one is under construction. Hard hat area..."

She chuckled and ushered Charlotte into her own office.

"Wow," said Charlotte stroking the back of one of the leather chairs. "Is this Restoration Hardware?"

Stephanie beamed. "It is."

"Really nice." Her gaze fell onto Lester's glass of bourbon. "Stress is getting to you, huh?"

Stephanie rolled her eyes. "You caught me." She moved to the glass and shifted it to the credenza, farther away from Charlotte.

"Is that bourbon?"

"Yes."

Charlotte chuckled. "Good thing Mariska's husband Bob didn't come with me. He loves bourbon. You'd be in trouble."

"Mm. Yes. *I'd* be in trouble."

"What kind is it?"

"Pappy Van Winkle."

"Is that a good one?"

Stephanie sighed. "Yes."

Charlotte looked at a yellow legal pad on the desk and walked around to grab a pen. "Mind if I write that down?" she asked, scrawling *Pappy Van Winkle* on the pad and ripping off the top sheet. She folded it and tucked it into the pocket of her shorts.

"Might make a good Christmas gift for Bob."

"Might. Great idea." Stephanie moved to lead Charlotte from the office. "Okay, well, I'll be back at your house in just a bit—"

"Your car was still at my house. Don't you need a ride? I can take you back." Charlotte glanced toward the closed shutters. "Is that car out there yours?"

"No."

"A new client?"

"Yes." Stephanie smiled. "Yes! He's in the bathroom. If you could skedaddle I'd really appreciate it—"

"In the bathroom all this time?" whispered Charlotte as Stephanie pushed her into the reception area. "That explains, well, I didn't want to say anything but there's a weird smell."

"Yes. He's got tummy issues. It's what he's suing about, actually."

"I thought you were a criminal lawyer."

"Uh, I moonlight. The occasional medical malpractice." She unlocked the bolt and pushed Charlotte toward sunlight.

Charlotte stepped outside and turned.

"Maybe I should stand guard until you wrap up? You know, keep an eye on the door at least?"

"No. No. I'll be fine. I'll be home in twenty minutes."

Charlotte grinned. "You called my house *home*."

Stephanie smiled and shut the door.

"But you don't have your car!" called Charlotte.

"That's why they invented Uber!"

Peeking through the shutters, she watched Charlotte get into her car and drive away. She strolled into her office, exhausted. Without thinking, she reached for the glass of bourbon on the credenza and had it to her lips before jerking it away, carefully rocking it to keep any from spilling. She hustled it to the bathroom and poured it down the sink. Opening the cabinet beneath, she grabbed a can of Comet and scrubbed the sink down with some wadded toilet paper. When she was done, she tossed the paper in the toilet and flushed.

What a day.

Stephanie went to the spare office, the glass tumbler in her hand. Lester was still immobile, one foot still on the wheelbarrow. She looked at the glass in her hand, looked at Lester, and then back again.

Pulling on his collar, she tucked the tumbler into his tucked-in t-shirt for safe keeping and pulled his car keys from his pocket. She hoisted him back into the wheelbarrow. She was happy he was such a small man. Jake was much larger.

She went outside, and after looking left and right for any sign of Charlotte, popped Lester's trunk. She propped open the front door with a law book, rolled the wheelbarrow to the back of the car and flipped Lester into the trunk. She rolled back to the spare office and with great effort, did the same with Jake.

Tucking in arms and legs, she closed and locked the car before returning the wheelbarrow to the side of the office.

"Time to go for a drive, boys," she mumbled, sliding into the driver's seat.

She knew right where to take them.

CHAPTER TWENTY-SEVEN

By the time Charlotte returned home, Declan and Seamus were waiting for her. Now, all three of them sat in her living room. It had been over an hour since she'd left Stephanie at her office.

"I really appreciate your help with this," said Charlotte, rubbing Declan's arm.

"You appreciate *my* help? You wouldn't even be in this mess if it wasn't for me."

"And your terrible taste in women," added Seamus.

Charlotte looked at Seamus and he offered her a crooked smile.

"Present company excluded, of course."

"*Thank you.*" Charlotte crooked her own mouth. "She said twenty minutes. I figured she'd be late with the client and his tummy issues, but I'm starting to think maybe we should go check on her."

"Where's your cat?" asked Declan.

"Carolina took him to Mariska's house for a visit. The two of them have developed some sort of bond."

"Witches and their familiars," mumbled Seamus.

Declan wandered to the front window and peered out.

"I see a car!" he said, stepping outside onto the stoop. Charlotte and Seamus followed him.

Stephanie stepped out of the back of a black Cadillac and the car rolled off. She spotted Declan, registered surprise, smoothed her skirt and walked up the driveway.

"Were you worried about me?" she asked him.

"Charlotte was."

"So you drove over here? That's sweet." She spotted Seamus in the doorway. "Oh, and you brought Lucky Charms. How magically delicious."

"You might be a little sweeter to me if you knew I'd found you a safe place to stay."

Stephanie rolled her eyes. "*Thanks*. I've been *meaning* to thank you for this five-star nursing home."

"Not *here*," said Charlotte. "Seamus has a friend who works for Witness Protection."

Stephanie's mouth fell open. "Witness Protection? I'm not going into Witness Protection!"

"We're not saying you are. This Marshal offered to help and she's an unknown. Your mother won't be able to make any connection to her, so you'll be safe."

Stephanie crossed her arms over her chest and bounced the strap of her small purse from one finger. After a minute she sighed. "Fine. It has to be better than staying here in the animal kingdom." She looked at Declan. "Did you know she has a pet mole?"

"It's a *Sphinx*," said Charlotte.

"Get your things," said Declan. "We'll drive you

over there."

"Maybe Simone can help us figure out our next move," added Seamus as Stephanie walked past him to grab her suitcases.

Stephanie returned a few minutes later and they piled into Declan's car.

They drove out of Pineapple Port and down the street to Silver Lake. Seamus let the guard know they were on their way to see Simone and he gave them a temporary pass.

"If it isn't Parking Pass Pete!" said Charlotte, leaning across Stephanie to wave at the guard. Pete lived in Pineapple Port and had earned the nickname *Parking Pass* thanks to his security job at Silver Lake.

"Well, hello there, Charlotte," said Pete.

"For the *love of Pete*, do you know *every* old person in Florida?" asked Stephanie, pushing Charlotte back and away from her.

Charlotte grimaced and sat back. "*Really* going to miss you."

Declan drove to Simone's house and they headed up the stairs to her front door with Stephanie lagging behind. Seamus knocked and Simone answered.

"I brought the girl," he said.

"Come in." She threw a dishtowel over her shoulder as she led the way. "I have something on the stove. Make yourselves at home for a moment."

Simone slipped back into the kitchen as the others gathered in the living room. Stephanie dragged her first suitcase through the door and Seamus closed it behind her.

"Thanks for the help," she muttered.

"My pleasure."

"Seamus, could you help me with something in the kitchen?" called Simone from the other room in a thick French accent.

Seamus looked at Charlotte, who flashed him what she hoped was a look of disapproval.

He shrugged to imply he was helpless. "Sure," he called back and disappeared into the kitchen.

Simone appeared a few minutes later.

"Can I get anyone anything to drink?"

Stephanie gasped and all heads turned to look.

"Are you okay dear?" asked Simone. "You look pale."

"My...my foot," said Stephanie. "My ankle buckled a little. I'm okay now."

"You do look pale," said Charlotte. "Are you sure you're okay?"

"Yes, I think so. You know, I think I forgot something in the car—"

"*I don't think so*," said Simone, pulling a gun from behind her back. She pointed it at them. "Put your hands up where I can see them."

"What's this?" asked Declan, raising his hands.

"And where is Seamus?" asked Charlotte.

Simone reached up with her free hand and pulled the dark wig from her head, revealing blonde hair beneath pinned in a flat bun. She motioned the gun at Stephanie. "You too."

"Declan, I'd like you to meet my mother, Jamie Moriarty," said Stephanie, raising her hands.

Charlotte stared at the striking older woman pointing the gun at her chest. "Moriarty?" she asked, looking at Stephanie. "So you're technically Stephanie *Moriarty*?"

Stephanie shrugged. "I suppose so. For as long as I'm *alive*."

Charlotte closed her eyes. "You've *got* to be kidding me."

"What?"

"You know, the whole Sherlock's arch nemesis thing."

Stephanie scoffed. "My, don't we have an inflated sense of our detective abilities—"

"Shut up!" barked Jamie. "All of you. Empty your pockets to the floor."

Charlotte made a show of checking her pocket while trying to find a way to dial the phone inside. There wasn't much room to work, and she made a note to wear looser shorts in the future.

"Pull it out," said Jamie, nodding the gun in Charlotte's direction.

She pulled out her phone. "Can I throw it on the sofa? If I drop it on the hardwood it will break and I don't have insurance."

Jamie scowled. "On an iPhone? That's crazy."

Charlotte tossed her phone onto the sofa, trying her best to make it land face down. If a phone call was in progress, she didn't want to telegraph it.

Jamie walked past the group and stood behind

them.

"Eyes forward. Walk down the hall. First room on the right."

The three looked at each other and Declan took the lead. As they passed the entrance to the kitchen, Declan glanced to his right and paused. Tight on his heels, Charlotte followed his gaze and spotted Seamus splayed on the tile floor. She watched his back, hoping to see it rise and fall with his breath.

"Keep walking!" snapped Jamie.

Stephanie jumped forward and smacked into the back of Charlotte. Charlotte caught her balance against Declan and then followed him into the first room on the right.

The room was empty but for what looked like a ballet bar mounted waist high on one wall.

"Line up against the bar," said Jamie, motioning with the gun. Holding the weapon aloft in her left hand, she rummaged in the closet across from them, her gaze on them never wavering. After a moment, she pulled two pairs of handcuffs from the closet and threw them to Stephanie.

"Cuff them both to the bar."

Stephanie grabbed Charlotte's raised wrist and pulled it down until it was close enough to snap the cuffs to the bar.

"You maybe could have *argued* with her for a second," whispered Charlotte.

Stephanie ignored her and moved to Declan. Before she could cuff him, he grabbed her and pulled her arm behind her back.

"Ow!" she protested.

"Drop the gun or I'll snap her neck," he said, his arm around her throat.

"*She's* the one who wants me *dead*, genius," said Stephanie. "Remember?"

"You wouldn't kill her anyway," added Jamie, staring pointedly at Stephanie. "He's too nice, right? He's *Superman*."

"What's that supposed to mean?" Declan asked.

"Let's put it this way, Superman. Let her go or I'll shoot your girlfriend." Jamie moved the gun to point it at Charlotte.

Declan released Stephanie. She snapped the handcuffs shut on his wrist, locking him to the wall.

"Sorry." She turned to her mother. "Now what?"

Jamie sighed. "Now we talk. Come with me." She left the room.

Stephanie looked at Declan. "I won't let her hurt you," she whispered.

"Um, *hello*," said Charlotte, waving the hand that wasn't cuffed.

Stephanie turned and walked out of the room. "Of course; I'll do my best for you."

"And Seamus!" called Charlotte after her. She turned in time to see Declan slide his cuff to the end of the bar and begin tugging on it. It didn't budge.

"Help me," he said, grunting.

She slid beside him and they counted to three before yanking on the bar. Still, no movement.

"Does she have this thing anchored to the earth's core?" said Declan, panting from the effort.

"*Drop it or I'll break her neck*," said Charlotte, imitating Declan's tough-guy voice.

He rolled his eyes. "What was I supposed to do?"

She hugged him with her free arm. "I'm just kidding. It was a nice try. Thank you for not letting her shoot me just so you could break Stephanie's neck."

"Very funny. This is serious. This woman is the Puzzle Killer. She won't have any qualms about killing us."

"I know. I know. This is how I deal with stress."

"And what about Seamus? Could you see anything?"

"I think I saw him breathing. I didn't see any blood, did you?"

Declan shook his head. "No."

"Is it me, or did she have a French accent that has since disappeared?"

"Like her dark hair."

"What are we going to do?"

Declan kissed her on her upturned forehead.

"Really? We could die and I get the mom-checking-for-a-fever kiss?"

He leaned down and gave her a lingering kiss on the lips.

"This is how I deal with stress."

She smiled. "Thank you. Much better. Now, *pull?*"

He nodded and wrapped his hands around the end of the metal bar.

"Pull."

CHAPTER TWENTY-EIGHT

Following Jamie, Stephanie returned to the living room. As she passed the kitchen she saw that Seamus remained motionless on the floor.

Her mother stood behind the sofa, in front of the door, gun at her side. "We need to talk."

Stephanie scoffed. "I'd say."

"Let's make a deal. Help me get rid of the three in there and I won't kill you. Is body dumping covered by attorney-client privilege?"

Stephanie stared at her mother. "I can't trust you as far as I can throw you. I help you get rid of those three, and when we're done dumping them, you'll push *me* in behind them."

Jamie shook her head. "Look, I only told Alex I'd kill you to buy some time. I need to find and kill *him*."

Stephanie put her hands in her pockets and felt a smooth object. She felt the stress building inside her give way, as if the breeze ruffling the surface of her waters had suddenly died. She felt calm.

She noticed a liquor cabinet against the wall. "Do you have any more of that bourbon?"

"I'm sure I do."

Stephanie walked to the cabinet and retrieved a

bottle while her mother stood guardedly, a few feet away.

"Glasses?" she asked.

"Kitchen."

"Two?"

Jamie stared at her as if considering the offer. "Sure. I could use a drink."

Stephanie walked into the kitchen and, stepping over Seamus' motionless body, found two whiskey tumblers in the cabinet. She returned to the living room, poured, and handed one to her mother, who took it with the hand not holding the gun.

"Cheers," she said, holding up her glass.

Jamie tapped hers, raised the glass to her lips, and shot it back.

"Funny thing about death," said Stephanie after finishing.

"What's that?" Jamie set her empty glass on the cabinet.

"It makes you do things you never thought you would."

"What are you talking about?"

"Take Debbie, my adopted mother, for example. She hid all your secrets from me my entire life. I didn't know I was adopted. I didn't know my mother was alive. And I certainly didn't know my mother was the Puzzle Killer."

Jamie pursed her lips. "It's not the sort of thing we felt was appropriate to share with you."

"Naturally. But the thing is, *dying* Debbie was on *so* many drugs. Drugs that made her very chatty.

That's when she told me about you."

"So you knew I existed before Alex sent me to you?"

"I knew much more than that. When I went through Debbie's papers, I also discovered how to contact you myself. You know, that emergency number you gave her for when she needed money?"

"The money I gave her was for *you*."

"Right. I'm sure I got every penny. But imagine my surprise when I discovered that you were nearby." Stephanie grit her teeth. "You were right *here*. For *years*. And you *never* visited me."

"You weren't even in town most of that time. You were at school...and then you ran away with that golf pro—"

"I was here *most* of the time. I needed you, and you were *a few miles away*. This may come as a shock, but the on-again, off-again meth head you left me with wasn't exactly winning any Mother of the Year awards."

"She did her job—"

"And now I find out you're a Federal Marshal? A Federal Marshal who sent every sicko on the East Coast to the town where she hid her daughter?"

Jamie chuckled. "What better way to hide from the law but under its nose?" She sighed. "Look, we have a lot to do. Is there a point to this story?"

Stephanie nodded. "Oh there is...if you haven't figured it out already."

"Figured it out?" Jamie's head tilted and she squinted at her daughter. "You said you discovered how to contact me, but you never called me as my *daughter*. In fact, I contacted *you*, after seeing Alex's ad in the paper."

"Quite a coincidence, don't you think? That the guy trying to find you would use your *daughter* as a go between?"

"I, I assumed he'd found out about you *somehow*. It's the only reason I took him seriously—" Jamie's voice trailed off.

"Come on, use that big brain of yours, Mom. You can put the pieces of this puzzle together."

"It's something that's been bothering me. How could he have known about you? Did Debbie—?"

"The fact Debbie never did tell anyone is a miracle. You left me with a bit of a wild card there, but no. Not Debbie. She was terrified of you."

Jamie put her free hand over her open mouth. "*You?*"

"There we go."

"*You're* Alex?" Her gaze dropped to the floor and then rocketed back to meet her daughter's. "*You* killed someone with an *alligator?*"

Stephanie smiled. "This little knife didn't fall far from the drawer."

"No."

Jamie dropped the hand covering her mouth and Stephanie realized her mother had been hiding a smile of sheer delight. She couldn't have looked happier if she'd just won the lottery. Or whatever news might make her mother happy. Probably not the lottery. Maybe a shiny new knife or something.

Her mother pointed at her. "*You're Alex!*"

"I'm Alex."

"Stephanie! That's *wonderful!*"

Stephanie jumped as her mother moved forward and embraced her. She pulled away and took a step back.

"You think it's wonderful that I was taunting you? Blackmailing you?"

"Yes! But wait, how did you know my whole resume?"

"I followed you to your storage locker after you killed the landscaper."

"That was *you?*"

"That's where I found your journal."

Jamie grinned and slapped her thigh. "And my cypher key is *Stephanie.*"

"Yes. That made it easy. And how heartwarming."

"But why get my attention with murders when you could have contacted me any time?" She coughed and placed her hand on her chest.

"It was a test. You *failed.*"

"I failed because I didn't figure out it was you all along?" She looked around the room and wiped her brow. "Is it hot in here?"

"No. And *no*, you didn't fail because you didn't realize I was the killer. You failed because you agreed to *kill me* to save your own hide."

"In my defense, I didn't know how interesting you'd turn out to be. I even killed a guy for you. Sort of. Because you told me you wanted no harm to come to Charlotte."

"What are you babbling about?"

"Nevermind. It's a long story. I kept a baseball. I'll show you some time."

"Let's get back to the problems at hand. Bottom line—you were going to kill me."

Jamie shrugged. "Guilty as charged. You knew too much."

"I'm your *daughter*."

"I—" Jamie swallowed and a spasm rippled through her body. She reached for the cabinet and knocked her empty glass off the edge. It shattered on the tile floor.

Stephanie watched. "Something wrong?"

Jamie fell to her knees and the gun slipped from her hand. She looked up. "What have you done?"

Stephanie squatted and stared into her mother's watering eyes. She pulled the empty vial from her pocket. "I'm pretty good with poisons. That one's cyanide. Like it? Looks like I had just enough left, I wasn't sure."

"You—" Jamie shuddered. "But now I can teach you how to stay free, alive, we could be...partners—"

She collapsed forward, reaching for Stephanie's foot.

Stephanie took a step back. "I have a question for you, Mom."

Jamie rolled on her back, her eyes narrowing. "Then maybe you shouldn't have poisoned me," she whispered.

Stephanie's hands curled to fists on either side of

her body and she braced herself. "Why let me live at all?"

Her mother took a ragged breath. "What?"

"Why let me live at all? Why *have* a baby?"

A smile curled on Jamie's lips. "It was an accident. And then an experiment."

Stephanie crouched to better hear her mother's weakening voice. "An experiment in *what*?"

Her mother's eyes shifted to the left and she stared out the window for a moment before answering. "I wanted to know if a baby could make me *feel*."

Stephanie pushed the side of her mother's head with her finger to force her to make eye contact. "Should I assume since you gave me away that the experiment *failed*?"

Jamie nodded, her breath steady but belabored.

"Why give me away? Why not kill me? Toss me in a river?"

Stephanie thought her mother was choking. It took her a moment to register the sound was wheezy laughter. With her limited breath, Jamie had begun to chortle, her mouth open, smiling like a carnival clown.

"What's so funny?" asked Stephanie, rising anger causing her head to ring with a high-pitched whistle.

Jamie coughed and then stopped laughing long enough to answer.

"The hard part was over. And...and I thought you'd make a great organ donor." She burst into another cluster of coughs mixed with peals of laughter.

Stephanie felt the blood drain from her face. "You what?"

"You know, in *case*. A liver...a heart...a living donor...a not so living donor. We have a history of cancer in the family, you know."

"How would I know about my family?"

Laughter bounced inside Stephanie's skull. She stood and put her hands on either side of her head, covering her ears, trying to drown out her mother's merriment.

Even through her self-imposed ear muffs, Stephanie heard the crash in the back bedroom. She dropped her hands and oriented herself. She was in the living room. She looked down. Her mother was still, her chest unmoving, a smile still on her lips.

There was another crash.

Stephanie ran down the hall.

CHAPTER TWENTY-NINE

Charlotte and Declan were on their butts. They had succeeded in pulling the bar from the wall, but the chunk of wall that fell with it made it impossible to slide the cuffs off the end.

Declan kicked at the drywall from the end of the pipe as Stephanie ran into the room.

"Stephanie!" said Charlotte, spotting her.

Stephanie remained silent, staring at them. Her body was standing in front of them, but to Charlotte, it seemed her mind was elsewhere.

"Where's your mother?" asked Declan.

"She's..." Stephanie looked back toward the living room. "She's dead."

"Dead?" echoed Charlotte.

Stephanie looked at her. She cleared her throat and her lost expression hardened. "Hold on." She moved to the closet and searched the shelves there. "I'll find the key."

Declan continued to stomp at the end of the metal bar as Charlotte did her best to give her wrist slack to avoid the cuffs jerking at her flesh. The drywall gave way and they could see the metal plate attached to the end.

"That's not going to work," said Charlotte.

"Wait! I found it," said Stephanie. She moved to Declan and unlocked his cuffs. He rubbed his wrist and strode out of the room as Charlotte was released. She stood and followed Declan into the kitchen. He knelt beside Seamus, lifting his uncle and propping his torso against the kitchen cabinets. He slapped him on the cheeks.

"Seamus. Seamus. Wake up."

Seamus' head began rocking from side to side and he jumped, raising his fist to strike as his eyes popped open.

"Whoa! Whoa!" said Declan, throwing up his open palms and leaning back.

"Declan!" said Seamus. "Where am I?" He looked around. "*Simone.*"

Declan stood and held out a hand to help up his uncle.

"What happened?" asked Charlotte.

Seamus rubbed at his head. "She told me to turn around. Held a gun to my head and a rag to my face." He nodded toward the counter where a small brown bottle sat next to a green kitchen towel.

Charlotte bent down to peer at the label without touching the bottle. "Chloroform."

"Where is she?" asked Seamus.

All gazes moved to Stephanie, who stood just outside the kitchen in the hall.

"She's over here," she said.

She moved into the living room with the others in tow. As Stephanie cleared the sofa, she gasped.

"She's gone!"

Charlotte rounded the sofa and saw nothing but a broken tumbler on the floor.

"Avoid the glass on the floor," said Stephanie, holding out her arm to keep Charlotte from getting too close. "She tried to poison me. I saw her drop powder into the glass. I distracted her and switched the glasses."

"That's so *Princess Bride*," said Charlotte. She felt a twinge of jealousy that Stephanie had done something so cool.

"And she drank it?" asked Declan.

"Yes! She collapsed here. I thought she was dead. That's when I came to help you."

Stephanie stepped over the glass and peered out the front door. "Her car is gone."

Charlotte heard a familiar ring and realized her phone was on the sofa. She reached over and picked it up.

"Hello?"

"I think you butt dialed me," said Mariska. "I'm just calling you back."

"I did. Sort of. Sorry. I have to go. I'll talk to you in a bit."

Charlotte hung up and followed the others outside. She spotted something on the cement and trotted down the stairs to investigate. It was a small, clear vial. She dropped to her knees to read the marks on it.

"It says *amyl nitrate*," she called up to the porch.

"That's part of a cyanide antidote kit," said Seamus.

Declan looked at him. "How would you know that?"

"Long story."

"She had an antidote kit?" said Stephanie.

"If she had the cyanide in the first place to poison you, it makes sense she'd have an antidote kit, too," said Charlotte as she made her way back to the porch.

Stephanie nodded. "Right. Right. That makes sense."

"She's on the run now," said Seamus. "That should keep her mind off killing you for a while."

Stephanie nodded.

"What did she say to you?" asked Charlotte.

Stephanie held her gaze for several seconds.

"Stephanie?"

"Nothing." Her clenched jaw relaxed and she offered a tiny smile. "Nothing I didn't already know."

CHAPTER THIRTY

Jamie opened her storage locker. Her passports. Her driver's licenses. Her gun. All the things she'd squirrelled away in the event she needed to disappear in a hurry.

She still felt sick. She closed the door behind her and leaned against the wall, breathing slowly and deliberately to avoid vomiting. Stephanie's dosage had been light or she never would have made it to the emergency kit in her car. She'd played a little possum in the house. Nice of Declan and the blonde to steal her daughter's attention long enough for her to scurry away.

Her own daughter had tried to kill her.

Her daughter was just like her.

A protégée!

She smiled.

And to have a lawyer in the family; that was handy.

Of course, at the moment, it didn't seem that Stephanie was leaping at the chance to represent her but that would change. *Would* change. She just needed to win the girl over. Sure, Stephanie seemed mad now, but she was a broken girl with deep abandonment issues. She couldn't resist Mommy forever.

She *was* disappointed in herself that she hadn't sensed Stephanie's leanings, though. She'd been too occupied with her own ambivalence towards the girl; her own feelings...or lack thereof. A tiny part of her had wondered—worried, really—that when she met Stephanie as an adult she'd feel something for the girl. After all, how was she supposed to really appreciate her as a baby? As a screaming, poop machine?

But she didn't feel anything. Maybe a tiny sense of pride that she was so pretty. Other than that, Stephanie was a stranger to her like any other; useful until she wasn't. An alien like everyone else.

It *had* been nice to admit to her daughter that she was the Puzzle Killer. It'd been a surprise to find her daughter so accepting. Far from horrified, Stephanie seemed fascinated by the information. At the time she chalked it up to her innate sense of attorney-client privilege.

Looking back, it should have been her first clue.

Jamie flipped on the storage unit light and gathered what she needed to escape. She hummed. She couldn't remember the last time she felt so...*light*.

Motherhood had been an interesting experiment, though failed. But now, a payoff! A kindred spirit. She'd never met another like herself. Killers didn't have tradeshows and union meetings.

She'd had every intention of killing Stephanie once her usefulness had passed. She couldn't have someone out there who knew her secrets, even family. Plus, there was that sense of *embarrassment.* The idea that she had produced an unremarkable child. A child like any other.

But she hadn't.

Stephanie had tried to kill her.

Jamie reached to grab a backpack from the shelf and scowled.

Peeps' baseball was gone.

Hm. She looked around and noticed a tarp covering something three feet tall and about the same width in the back of the unit. She squinted at it.

How had she not seen that? Even behind the clutter of furniture, it should have been the first thing she noticed amiss.

I really have to get myself together.

She crawled her way over an old sofa and lifted the tarp to reveal two blue oil drums.

These are not mine.

She scanned the unit. Nothing else seemed odd. She peered around the barrels, searching for traps. A person could fit a lot of explosive in two oil drums.

Nothing.

She really didn't have time for this nonsense. She needed to leave. But...

She unscrewed the cap of the drum on the left and was accosted by a putrid smell. She slapped the cap back on. Holding her hand over her nose, she pried at the lid until it popped off and fell to the ground beside her.

Inside, was the folded body of a large man, his

arms covered in tattoos.

Jamie picked up the lid and replaced it.

The only person who knew about her storage unit was Stephanie.

She pulled out her phone and called the front office to ask if anyone had been to her unit.

"Hold on," said the man on the line. "Gotta look up the sign-in. What day?"

"I don't know exactly. In the last week?"

"Nope."

"Well that's a lie. Someone's been in here!"

"Would you like to file a complaint?" His tone told her how much he cared.

Jamie sighed.

The interloper had to have been Stephanie, pinning her bodies on the Puzzle Killer.

Brilliant.

She liked this kid more and more.

"Mam?"

"No. I'm mistaken. Nevermind."

Jamie hung up. She felt as though she should ream the man for letting someone sneak into her unit, but she didn't have the time. And she was too darn *happy*.

She also didn't want the deskman stopping by her unit. She had to leave. No time to dump the bodies.

"You win this one, daughter," she said.

She couldn't stop smiling.

CHAPTER THIRTY-ONE

Charlotte, Mariska and Darla sat in Darla's kitchen sipping coffee. It had been two days since Stephanie's mother, a.k.a. Jamie Moriarty, a.k.a. Simone, a.k.a. the Puzzle Killer, had disappeared.

Frank walked in to enjoy his pre-lunch lunch.

"Have you heard anything new?" asked Charlotte, jumping from her seat at the sight of him.

Frank grabbed a muffin from a plastic tray.

"Not much. Her house was clean if you don't count handcuffs and leather masks." He rolled his eyes. "Nothing else useful except the conversation between her and that other killer on the computer."

"The conversation about killing Stephanie?"

He nodded. "Yup. Her and Alex, back and forth. His email was Alex alligator at Viagra pills dot com or something crazy."

"But no leads on him?"

"Nah. Nothing solid. The nerds are still tearing apart the computer so maybe something will pop up."

"Poor Stephanie," said Mariska. "I can't imagine discovering that my mother wanted to kill me."

Darla shrugged. "Mine always said she wanted to kill me, but I knew she was kidding." She tilted her head. "Pretty sure, anyway."

"Did you see this?" Mariska asked, handing Charlotte the paper. On the cover was a photo of Stephanie, looking sad yet determined. *Lawyer Nearly Captures the Puzzle Killer* said the headline.

"She didn't nearly capture her, she nearly *killed* her," mumbled Charlotte, scanning the story. She was still a little bitter about Stephanie's opportunity to *Princess Bride* someone. The paper told the story of Stephanie's capture at gunpoint, the poison, and Jamie Moriarty's escape from the police.

"Why aren't you in that story?" asked Darla.

Charlotte shrugged. "No one asked. This story is all about *Stephanie's* harrowing experience. I'm guessing she went to the press and left us out, for which I am eternally grateful."

"Why? You were there when the Puzzle Killer was nearly captured. Wouldn't that be good for business?"

"I was cuffed to a wall and my mentor was unconscious on the kitchen floor. I don't think that colors us in the best light."

"*Mentor,*" muttered Frank, shoving the last of the muffin in his maw. "This whole thing is just a bunch of extra paperwork for me. Gonna drive me to drink."

"Oh! That reminds me!" said Charlotte, pulling a folded piece of yellow lined paper from her pocket. "Stephanie had some very high-end bourbon at her office. I wrote down the name of it for you." She opened up the sheet and handed it to Frank.

He looked at it and laughed. "Pappy VanWinkle's one of the most expensive bourbons in the world! She had it at her office?"

"Yep."

"Hm. I might need a law consult sometime soon." Frank tossed the sheet on the table and put on his hat. "I'll see you ladies later."

Frank left and Charlotte let her gaze drift to the lined legal paper. The late morning sun gleamed through the kitchen window and hit the paper at an angle that allowed her to see the indentation of past notes written on the sheets above. She recognized the one word as an email.

GatorAlex@erectionpillz.com

Alex.

She straightened. "Alex was talking to Jamie through the computer."

Mariska nodded. "Frank said Alex. I remember the name because when he said it, I pictured someone emailing Alex Trebek."

"Me too!" said Darla.

"I have to go," said Charlotte. "Can I borrow your car?"

"Sure," said Mariska. "We're just going to join Carolina at the pool in a bit."

"She went without you? Why didn't she wait?"

"I think she's looking for Lester," said Darla, winking.

"Oh, she is *not*," said Mariska.

"I hope not. We haven't found out what they arrested him for yet."

"He's probably in jail," said Charlotte.

"He hasn't been around. He was lurking at Carolina's side night and day, and now he's nowhere to be found."

"That's why Carolina is pining for him," said Darla.

"Stop that!" said Mariska. "You'll start rumors. Anyway it's worse than Lester. She took the cat with her. Has him on a leash and bought him a little sun cover-up and a visor."

Charlotte shook her head and headed for the door.

Charlotte drove to Stephanie's office. She spotted the blonde standing outside, supervising the men hanging a new sign on her building. A sign that said, *Moriarty Law.*

She parked and walked to Stephanie's side.

"Nice sign."

"Isn't it?" said Stephanie. "I think the navy shows strength."

"*Moriarty*, the villain from Sherlock Holmes and the last name of the Puzzle Killer. Are you sure that's the image you want to go with?"

"You forget, it's my real last name."

"Still..."

Stephanie smiled. "I'm a criminal defense lawyer. I could call it Lex Luthor Law and it would only help."

Charlotte nodded. "Gotcha. Could I talk to you a second? Inside?"

Stephanie looked at her. "Sure."

They made their way inside the office.

Charlotte took the opportunity to sit in the gorgeous leather chair across from Stephanie's desk. She found herself eye level with the credenza against the wall. There was a baseball in a glass trophy box that hadn't been there before.

"Baseball fan?" she asked, standing again to approach it.

"Hate it."

Charlotte leaned over to inspect the ball. There was no signature on it.

"It's just blank?"

Stephanie stared at her. "Did you come here to inspect my baseball?"

Charlotte scowled. "No...I guess I'll get right to the point."

"Too late."

"I imagine you have a press schedule to keep today."

"I do."

"Of course. Anyway, does the email *GatorAlex@erectionpillz.com* mean anything to you?"

Stephanie's face remained unchanged. "Seriously? No. I haven't used erection pills in months."

"That address was indented on the sheet of paper I borrowed from you when I was here the other day."

Stephanie shrugged. "Don't know what to tell you."

"What if I told you *that* address was the address they pulled from your mother's computer. It's how she spoke with the person blackmailing her."

"Fascinating."

"So you can't imagine how that address would end up on your desk?"

"I don't think it was."

"I just told you it was on the paper I borrowed from you."

"Are you sure? You were in my mother's house, after all. Maybe you picked it up there."

"It says Pappy Van Winkle on it!"

"So?"

Charlotte sighed. "I think you know who was talking to your mother. I think you arranged their conversation."

"Even if I did, I really can't discuss my mother's case."

"I think you know who the other killer is."

Stephanie stared at her, silent.

"Fine," said Charlotte, folding the paper and putting it back in her pocket. She stood. "But I'm telling you now, I think you know a lot more than you're letting on. You might even know where your mother went."

"I wish I did. She's trying to kill me, you know. I'm the victim here." Stephanie walked past Charlotte and sat at her desk. "Now if you wouldn't mind, I have a lot of work."

Charlotte left the office and returned to her car. She sat there for a moment, staring at the new sign.

The parking place beside her triggered a memory. *A car.* There had been a car at Stephanie's office the last time she was here.

A client. Stephanie said there was a client in her bathroom. Maybe that client was the mysterious Alex.

She squeezed her eyes tight, but she couldn't conjure an image of the license plate. She tapped the side of her head with her hand, trying to remember. A maroon Cadillac. Numbers...she wanted to say the license plate had a lot of numbers as oppose to letters: three, four...

Arg! She couldn't remember. Seamus would be so disappointed.

She turned the ignition. Maybe she'd be able to remember in the shower. She remembered a lot of things in the shower. There and in bed. Maybe she could dream the license plate.

She left and pulled into Pineapple Port, rolling through the older section on her way home. She looked left as she passed Alpinia Lane and saw it.

A maroon Cadillac.

She slammed on the brakes and slipped the car into reverse.

That was it. She was *sure* of it. Same shape, same rust pattern over the back tire, and the license plate was 3462MN.

It was sitting in Lester's driveway, like it had been there forever.

Lester was Alex?
Lester was Alex!

It made sense. Lester had only been in town a couple of months. He was renting, like he had come for a particular purpose. What had he told Carolina at the pool? That he was here on business? What business?

Charlotte scrambled for her phone and dialed Frank's number. He answered.

"Hello?"

"Frank! Lester is Alex!"

"What?"

"Lester. Lester is the *killer*. Alex. The one blackmailing Stephanie's mom."

She heard Frank sigh. "I know."

"You know? How do you know?"

"Because we just found him."

"You got him? That's great!"

"Not great for him. He's dead."

Charlotte gasped. "Dead?"

"Stuffed in a barrel in a storage locker, along with another fella we haven't identified. The locker belongs to Jamie Moriarty."

"Her name is on it?"

"Not officially. She used an alias. But they found the storage unit information at her house. Look, we're in the middle of this mess right now. I'll talk to you about it later, okay?"

"Okay."

Charlotte hung up.

Lester *was* Alex and the Puzzle Killer had gotten to him first.

It had to be. It made sense. Stephanie had acted

as the connection between her mother and Lester.

Right?

Charlotte put her car back in drive and rolled toward home.

It made sense...

...didn't it?

CHAPTER THIRTY-TWO

"What a week," said Charlotte. "You know, after all these murders, they found the poor landscaping guy from my neighborhood dead in his backyard? Accidentally cut his leg open with a machete and bled to death."

"Really? That's awful," said Declan.

Charlotte lay on a bed in the Hock o' Bell Pawnshop, exhausted. She'd been visiting Declan when he decided to swing back to the store and make sure Blade's shift had gone well. She joined him.

"Wait." She sat up. "No one died on this bed, did they?"

"No. That's a new one," said Declan, flipping through the receipts. "It's a guest bed of someone who never had any guests. Under the new sheets I put on it there's still plastic."

She bounced up and down and heard the crinkling of plastic.

"Good." She flopped back down.

"Did the cat carrier fit?" he asked.

"I guess so. Auntie Carolina is back in Michigan and Mr. Coppertone the naked cat went with her. She couldn't bear to leave him behind and I didn't really need a cat, so it all worked out for the best."

Declan walked over and laid down next to her. "On the upside, looks like Blade hasn't killed anyone yet. He seems to be doing a great job. Even though I can't figure him out. I had a customer gush about him. *Him*."

"He's a strange fellow."

"That's one way to put it. Did you see what he was wearing? A red polo shirt two sizes too large and dayglow orange cargo shorts."

"I saw! What's up with that?"

"It's his new work uniform, apparently. I told him not to wear t-shirts, so he returned in a tank top, and when I shot that down he wore the giant polo-tent. I'm terrified to tell him that doesn't work either, for fear he'll show up wrapped in human skin."

They heard the sound of someone clearing their throat and sat bold upright.

Blade was standing at the foot of the bed.

"Blade!" said Declan. "I thought you'd left!"

"Had to hit the head," he said, thumbing toward the bathroom in the back.

"Okay, well, you can go now. Use the back door. I already locked up the front."

He nodded and shuffled off.

"Do you think he heard us?" whispered Charlotte.

Declan sighed. "I don't know. How did he get to the foot of the bed without us seeing him?"

Charlotte chuckled. "Hey, I have a question for you."

"Uh oh."

"Why do you think Stephanie is so obsessed with you?"

He held up a hand. "Isn't it obvious?"

She slapped him lightly on the chest. "Seriously."

He sighed. "I don't know. We grew up together. I knew she had this, I don't know, *awful* side to her, but for some reason she never used her powers of evil against me. She was bullied in school and the fact that she retaliated tenfold didn't help. But I thought she was smart and funny and we got along."

"Until you dated."

"Until we dated. I should have seen that coming. But even then, I dunno..."

"What?"

"It's like she didn't really want to blow things up but she *had* to."

"Do you think she thinks you're the only person who appreciates the real her?"

He shrugged. "I don't know. Why are we talking about Stephanie anyway?"

"Because something is fishy. I can't stop thinking about how everything happened. With Lester the most likely person to be Alex and Steph's mom being the Puzzle Killer; something isn't right and I *know* Stephanie knows more than she's telling."

"I think that's always the case with her."

"Lester was *tiny*. How did he get that enormous alligator in that pool?"

"I guess he had help. What about the guy in the barrel next to him you told me about?"

"Maybe. But what's the connection between

Lester and Jamie?"

"Maybe the other guy is the connection. Maybe *he's* Alex and Lester relayed his messages to Stephanie?"

"Maybe they're both Jamie's victims. Maybe neither one is Alex. *Anyone could be Alex...*"

Declan rolled on his side to face Charlotte. "I hate it when you trail off like that. What are you thinking now?"

"I'm wondering if Stephanie would ever kill someone."

"What?"

"Seriously. Do you think she could kill someone?"

"I—" He sighed. "My first instinct is to say no, of course. But, I guess I'd have to know the circumstances of this hypothetical murder situation."

"How about a situation where her mother abandons her as a baby and then shows up years later as the Puzzle Killer?"

"You think *Stephanie* is Alex? She killed people to catch her mother's attention?"

"You have to admit, she has more motive than—"

Declan put his arm over her and kissed her on the lips.

"Sshhh," he mumbled.

"But don't you—"

He kissed her again, lingering. Charlotte felt her body relax as his hand traced the side of her body.

"So you're saying I need to let it go?" she

whispered.

He nodded. "Let the cops look into things. They'll find the connection between Lester and Jamie eventually."

Charlotte sighed. "I guess you're right."

Declan kissed her again and stood. He held out his hand to help her up. "Anyway, if anyone killed anyone around here, it has to be Blade," he said.

"Blade is Alex! Of course!" she said, letting him pull her to her feet.

"I mean, *come on*. Nobody that odd named *Blade* is *not* a killer." Declan wrapped her into a hug. "He's probably got bodies stacked at home like—"

The sound of a throat clearing echoed through the store. They whipped their gazes toward the sound and found Blade standing four feet from them.

"Blade!" yelped Declan, his voice cracking. "What are you doing here?"

"Forgot my lunch kit," he said, holding up an old metal lunch box.

Charlotte found herself transfixed by the metal box in Blade's hand. Painted on the side, three grinning, disembodied women's heads floated over the title *Charlie's Angels*.

"See you tomorrow, boss." Blade turned to leave. After a moment, they heard the backdoor click shut behind him.

"How long do you think he was there?" whispered Charlotte. She could feel giggles building inside of her.

Declan shook his head. "The next time I get the idea to hire someone, kick me, will you?"

THE END

Thank you for taking time to read *Pineapple Puzzles!* If you enjoyed it, please consider telling your friends or posting a review on Amazon or GoodReads or wherever you like to roam. Word of mouth helps poor starving authors so much!

To keep up with what I'm writing next, visit my humor blog/author site and sign up for my newsletter at:

http://www.AmyVansant.com

Twitter:
https://twitter.com/AmyVansant

Facebook:
https://www.facebook.com/TheAmyVansant

For questions or delightful chit-chat:
Amy@AmyVansant.com

ABOUT THE AUTHOR

Amy has been writing and finding other creative ways to make no money since high school.

She specializes in fun, comedic reads about accident prone, easily distracted women with questionable taste in men.

So, autobiographies, mostly.

Amy is the former East Coast Editor of *SURFER Magazine* but the urge to drive up and down the coast interviewing surfers has long since left her. She works at home with her goofy husband.

She *has* rocked water aerobics at a fifty-five and over community, but has yet to play bingo. She's heard it's vicious.

OTHER BOOKS BY AMY VANSANT

Pineapple Port Mysteries
Funny, mysteries full of unforgettable characters
Pineapple Lies (I) Pineapple Mystery Box (II)
Pineapple Puzzles (III) Pineapple Land War (IV)
Pineapple Beach House (V) Pineapple Disco (VI)
Pineapple Gingerbread Men (VII) Pineapple Jailbird (VIII)

Kilty Romantic Comedy/Thrillers
Funny, suspenseful romance - touch of time-travel
Kilty as Charged (I) Kilty Conscience (II) Kilty Mind

(III) Kilty as Sin (IV)

Angeli Urban Fantasy
Thrilling adventures with a touch of romantic comedy
Angeli (I) Cherubim (II) Varymor (III)

Slightly Romantic Comedies
New Adult/Adult zany romantic romps
Slightly Stalky (I) Slightly Sweaty (II)

The Magicatory (middle-grade fantasy)
Moms are Nuts (editor: humor anthology)
The Surfer's Guide to Florida (non-fiction: out of print)

CPSIA information can be obtained
at www.ICGtesting.com
Printed in the USA
LVHW051521280420
654675LV00018B/1690